Praise for Kate Hoffmann's Mighty Quinns

"This truly delightful tale packs in the heat and a lot of heart at the same time."
—*RT Book Reviews* on *The Mighty Quinns: Dermot*

"This is a fast read that is hard to tear the eyes from. Once I picked it up I couldn't put it down."
—*Fresh Fiction* on *The Mighty Quinns: Dermot*

"A story that not only pulled me in, but left me weak in the knees."
—*Seriously Reviewed* on *The Mighty Quinns: Riley*

"Sexy, heartwarming and romantic, this is a story to settle down with and enjoy—and then reread."
—*RT Book Reviews* on *The Mighty Quinns: Teague*

"Sexy Irish folklore and intrigue weave throughout this steamy tale."
—*RT Book Reviews* on *The Mighty Quinns: Kellan*

"The only drawback to this story is that it's far too short!"
—*Fresh Fiction* on *The Mighty Quinns: Kellan*

"Strong, imperfect but lovable characters, an interesting setting and great sensuality."
—*RT Book Reviews* on *The Mighty Quinns: Brody*

Blaze®

Dear Reader,

One of my favorite things about writing books for Harlequin is the opportunity to explore interesting new places. When I decided to do this latest quartet of Mighty Quinn books, I was excited to have the chance to choose four very different settings, in various parts of the world. Of course, the final book had to be set in Ireland, but for this book, I played with the settings of Central America and Africa before deciding on the island of Cape Breton in Canada.

With its vibrant Celtic culture and old lighthouses, I knew right away that this was the perfect place for a Quinn to fall in love—with the countryside and the heroine!

So, for all my Canadian fans, this one's for you. I hope I've represented this beautiful corner of your country well. I think it's the perfect place for Rourke and Annie to find their happy ending.

Enjoy!

Kate Hoffmann

The Mighty Quinns: Rourke

Kate Hoffmann

ISBN-13: 978-0-373-79772-1

THE MIGHTY QUINNS: ROURKE

This edition published by arrangement with Harlequin Books S.A.

For questions and comments about the quality of this book, please contact us at CustomerService@Harlequin.com.

Printed in U.S.A.

ABOUT THE AUTHOR

Kate Hoffmann has written more than seventy books for Harlequin, most of them for the Temptation and Blaze lines. She spent time as a music teacher, a retail assistant buyer and an advertising exec before she settled into a career as a full-time writer. She continues to pursue her interests in music, theater and musical theater, working with local schools in various productions. She lives in southeastern Wisconsin with her cat, Chloe.

Books by Kate Hoffmann

HARLEQUIN BLAZE

279—THE MIGHTY QUINNS: MARCUS
285—THE MIGHTY QUINNS: IAN
291—THE MIGHTY QUINNS: DECLAN
340—DOING IRELAND!
356—FOR LUST OR MONEY
379—YOUR BED OR MINE?
406—INCOGNITO
438—WHO NEEDS MISTLETOE?
476—THE MIGHTY QUINNS: BRODY
482—THE MIGHTY QUINNS: TEAGUE
488—THE MIGHTY QUINNS: CALLUM
520—THE CHARMER
532—THE DRIFTER
546—THE SEXY DEVIL
579—IT MUST HAVE BEEN THE MISTLETOE...
"When She Was Naughty..."
585—INTO THE NIGHT
641—THE MIGHTY QUINNS: RILEY
647—THE MIGHTY QUINNS: DANNY
653—THE MIGHTY QUINNS: KELLAN
675—BLAZING BEDTIME STORIES, VOLUME VI
"Off the Beaten Path"
681—NOT JUST FRIENDS
702—THE MIGHTY QUINNS: DERMOT
707—THE MIGHTY QUINNS: KIERAN
712—THE MIGHTY QUINNS: CAMERON
719—THE MIGHTY QUINNS: RONAN
735—THE MIGHTY QUINNS: LOGAN
746—THE MIGHTY QUINNS: JACK

HARLEQUIN SINGLE TITLES

REUNITED
THE PROMISE
THE LEGACY

Dedicated to the memory of Rita MacNeil,
an extraordinary voice from an extraordinary place.

Prologue

"IT'S BEEN SO long. I'm beginning to lose hope that we'll ever find them."

Aileen Quinn stared out the window of her office at the slate-gray sky. Autumn was quickly turning to winter and she dreaded the damp cold that would settle into her bones. In her younger days, she'd traveled to the south of France during the worst of the Irish winter, soaking up the sun along the Mediterranean coast. But she hadn't traveled for years, finding herself more comfortable in familiar surroundings.

"I have one more lead to check on your brother Diarmuid," Ian said, leafing through his notes. "But I'm sad to say that we've found nothing on Lochlan. I have researchers on four continents looking for him, but he just disappeared. Off the grid, they call it."

Aileen had hired Ian Stephens months ago to

help her research the parents she'd never known for a chapter in her autobiography. She had grown up in an orphanage, believing that she'd been the only daughter of a destitute Irish widow who'd died of consumption—after her husband had been killed in the Easter Uprising. But Ian had discovered four older brothers—siblings she hadn't remembered—whose fates had been scattered to the winds when their mother couldn't care for them.

"I'm another year older," Aileen said. She forced a bright smile. "I never intended to live to see my ninety-seventh birthday. Good Lord, I've lived far too long."

"You're the youngest ninety-seven-year-old I've ever met," Ian said with a smile. "Look at you. You're still writing, still active."

"That's lovely of you to say, but it doesn't make this old body of mine feel any younger." Aileen laughed softly. "In my mind, I'm still a young woman. When I look in the mirror these days, I barely recognize myself. I wish I could have some of those years back."

"You've led a full life, Miss Quinn. An important life. Your books have meant a lot to so many people. You're one of Ireland's most beloved novelists."

"And yet, I'm searching the ends of the earth for a family, desperate to give myself a legacy beyond my books. I could have had my own family if I hadn't put my work first."

Ian had found the descendants of two of her brothers—Tomas's family near Brisbane, Australia, and Conal's family in Chicago in the U.S. But it had been five months since he'd brought good news about the other two. She'd planned a festive family reunion for the holidays at Ballyseede Castle, leasing out the entire castle and its twenty-two bedrooms. She wanted the rooms full.

"What do you know of Diarmuid so far?" Aileen asked.

"We've come across a clue in a 1945 Canadian census. The age seems to be right and the individual lists his birthplace as Ireland. His name is registered as Dermot, but that is the anglicized version of the Gaelic name. Sometimes the census takers didn't always get a spelling correct."

Aileen leaned forward in her chair. "That does sound hopeful."

"If this Dermot is the one, he settled on Cape Breton, worked as a fisherman and had three sons. The eldest, Alistair, died in the Second World War. The next son, Brian, or Buddy, as he was known, died about five months ago, a bachelor. And the youngest, Paul, died about eight years ago. His son, Rourke, is the only heir."

"Rourke?"

"From our research, that's his mother's maiden

name. She was quite a bit younger than her husband and has since remarried."

"When will we know for sure if Dermot is Diarmuid?" Aileen asked.

"It's difficult to say. But we're getting closer. I have a genealogist in Halifax who will be traveling to Cape Breton this week to check the records and ask some questions. Hopefully someone will remember something about Dermot."

A soft knock sounded on the door and Sally stepped inside Aileen's office. "I have lunch laid out in the breakfast room whenever you're ready, ma'am."

"Thank you, Sally," Aileen replied. "We'll be along in a bit." She turned to Ian. "I hope you'll stay. I wanted to tell you about my plans for a grand family reunion over the Christmas holidays. I've rented a castle."

Ian blinked in surprise. "A castle? Well, in that case, I'm not sure I should pause for lunch. I have a lot to accomplish over the next few months."

"Of course, I want you to be there," Aileen said. "I want you to put together a book on the family history. The reunion will be the final chapter in my autobiography."

"It would make a perfect ending."

"Much better than a funeral, don't you think?" Aileen teased. She pushed up from her chair, wincing at the ache in her hip. "Come," she said. "Let's see what Sally has for us. I smelled bread baking this morning."

Ian circled her desk and held out his arm. Aileen took it, clutching her cane in her other hand. "Did I tell you someone at the RTE network contacted me when they learned about our search?" he asked. "They have an American production company that wants to make a documentary about your life."

"Imagine that," Aileen said. "I can't think it would be a very interesting documentary."

"I beg to differ," Ian said. "I think it would be wonderful. And that's what I told the producer when she called me."

"Oh, I don't know," Aileen said. "I've managed for so long to keep a private life. You don't think a documentary might be…unseemly, do you?"

"I think your readers would love to know more about the woman behind the books."

"I'll have to think about that," Aileen said. "Perhaps you can convince me over lunch." They walked out into the foyer. "And we can discuss hiring more investigators to search out Lochlan. One just doesn't go missing in the modern world. There's always something left behind, some piece of paper that will give us a clue. Perhaps if we find Diarmuid, that branch of the family will know about Lochlan."

"We'll fill those twenty-two bedrooms in Ballyseede Castle," Ian said. "Mark my words."

"Yes. I believe we will," Aileen replied.

1

THE PEARSON BAY hardware store was bustling with activity as Rourke Quinn walked through the battered front door. The locals, worried about the approaching storm, were buying last-minute supplies before the wind and rain drove them indoors.

"Hey, Rourke! You hanging around for this? It's supposed to be the storm of the decade. At least that's what forecasters are callin' it."

Rourke turned to smile at Betty Gillies, the store owner. "Nope. I'm heading out. I want to get to the mainland before it hits. I just needed some batteries for my camera. Thought I'd take a few last pictures of the coastline before I left the island."

"We're going to miss you around here," she said. "Heck, I'm gonna miss you. You were good for the bottom line."

Rourke chuckled. "I'm sure I was."

He'd arrived on the eastern shore of Cape Breton Island almost three months ago, coming to the Maritimes to settle his uncle's estate. His father's family had lived on the island for almost a hundred years, plying the waters of the Atlantic as fishermen. But Uncle Buddy was the last of the Quinns to make his home on Cape Breton and now that he was gone, his cottage would be sold.

Born in America of an American mother and a Canadian father, Rourke had always felt torn between the Cape Breton culture of his Canadian family and the big-city life of his hometown. His uncle had known this and Rourke suspected that was why the cottage had been left to him—so that he might find his way "home" again.

Rourke had spent summer vacations working on his uncle's fishing boat, making the long trip up from New York City, where his parents lived. His father, Paul, had wanted Rourke to experience a working-class job, hoping that it would make him more interested in college and a business career. As he got older, Rourke found himself drawn to the business Paul had founded with two friends. During high school, he spent his summer vacations with his father, learning the ins and outs of civil engineering. Uncle Buddy was relegated to a couple weeks at the end of August.

Rourke felt a familiar twinge of guilt assail him,

but he brushed it aside. He'd spent the past three months renovating Buddy's place, making it habitable for a modern family. Now it was ready. He'd talked to a few real estate agents and made plans to list it, but he hadn't made a final decision. Perhaps it might be better to rent it out.

"A single decision can change the course of your life," he murmured to himself. Buddy had always offered sage advice with pithy sayings or old proverbs. That was one of his favorites.

When Rourke was young he used to tease his uncle. *Yeah, I'll make sure to embroider that on a pillow,* he'd say. But now that he was older, he'd begun to realize the impact of that advice—and the truth of it as it applied to his own life.

After high school, he'd decided to join the firm. He worked nights and weekends as a draftsman at Paul's office and took engineering classes during the day. Though it was never said out loud, he knew that the company was in trouble and that his father needed his help. And with every year that passed, the stress took more of a toll on Paul's health.

He'd continued to work at the company, even after his father's sudden death of a heart attack, hoping to save his dad's legacy by getting the firm back on track. But without the support of the other two partners, Rourke knew it was a lost cause. He quit the day after he heard of Buddy's death.

Rourke stared at the selection of batteries. He wished he'd had one last chance to talk to Buddy, to ask him the questions that had been plaguing him for the past few years. *Where is my life going? What do I really want? Am I ever going to be truly satisfied?*

"So you're putting the place up for sale, are you?" Betty asked.

"I haven't decided yet," Rourke replied as he pulled a package of batteries off the rack and dropped it on the counter. "I don't want to make any hasty decisions."

"Is this it?" she said, pointing to the batteries.

Rourke nodded, then reached into his pocket for his wallet. But as he was pulling out the money to pay for the purchase, the patrons around him suddenly went silent. Betty's gaze fixed on a spot over his shoulder and Rourke slowly turned.

Annie Macintosh was a familiar figure to everyone in town. Her family had lived on the eastern shore as long as the Quinns had. Her great-grandfather had built and kept the lighthouse on Freer's Point.

Annie's life had been more tragic than most. Her parents had died when she was young, both of them drowned under mysterious circumstances. She'd been brought up by her grandmother in the old light keeper's cottage, set on a beautiful piece of property overlooking the Atlantic.

As a shy child, she'd been the target of the local bullies, their taunts focused on her stammer, on her mismatched clothes, on her tangled auburn hair or her pale complexion. Recalling the torment as an adult, Rourke had to wonder why no one had stepped in to help her. He'd stood up for her once, only to get pummeled for it by a group of six townies.

He could see her now, surrounded by the six bullies, her stance defiant, struggling to express her anger even through her stutter, which invited more derision from the boys. It had been the most courageous thing he'd seen in his young life and it had been one of those moments that Buddy had talked about. That day, he'd realized that he wouldn't spend his life being led by others. He was a leader, not a follower.

Annie silently walked to the row of freezers and refrigerators on the far wall that held bait for the sport fishermen. When she returned to the counter, she was carrying two large boxes of frozen herring.

Rourke stepped aside, giving her a hesitant smile. "Go ahead. I can wait."

She smiled back at him and for a moment, Rourke forgot to breathe. The dirty, disheveled girl had grown into an incredible beauty. Her eyes had always been an odd shade of blue—almost teal—ringed with dark lashes, but they had an unexpected effect on him now. Her hair, thick and wavy, hung just to her shoulders, and though tousled by the wind, seemed to be well tended. She wore simple clothes, a pair of jeans that hugged her long legs, a faded shirt and a canvas jacket.

But it was that heart-shaped face, so unusual and so captivating. He couldn't seem to bring himself to look away. He took in as many details as he could before she finished her transaction. After she paid, she hefted the two boxes into her arms and turned for the door.

"Thank you," she murmured softly, her gaze meeting his and then lingering for a moment. The corners of her mouth curled up slightly in what he could only take as a hesitant smile.

Somehow, he sensed that her gratitude wasn't for the cut in line, but for what had happened all those years ago. "Can I help you carry those out?" he asked, reaching for the box under her left arm.

She shook her head and tried to walk by him, twisting her body away. The box slipped from her grasp and hit the floor with a thud, then slid across the hardwood like a giant hockey puck.

Rourke made a move to retrieve it, but so did she, and when they reached the frost-covered box, they bumped heads as they squatted at the same time. He grabbed the box, then helped her to her feet. "Where are you parked?" he asked.

Cursing beneath her breath, she took the box

from him, struggling as she tried to tuck it under her arm. Then, without giving him another look, she turned and hurried out of the store. Rourke stared after her, speechless, wondering at her odd behavior. The rest of the patrons had watched her retreat in silence, as well.

Drawing a deep breath, he returned to the counter and laid out the money for the batteries. "That was odd," he murmured.

"You're tellin' me," Betty replied.

"What do you think she's going to do with all that herring?"

"The locals use it for crab pots," Betty said. "But that's not what's odd."

"What is, then?"

"I don't think I've ever heard her speak."

Rourke frowned. "Really? I know as a kid she didn't say much, but I hadn't realized that was still going on."

"She doesn't talk to anyone. Just goes about her business. Gotta wonder about that. She must get a little lonely out there, living all by herself." Betty made a little circle with her finger beside her temple. "Some of us think all that solitude has made her a bit crazy."

"I haven't been out to the Freer's Point light in years," Rourke said. "Not sure I could find it if I tried."

"You take the turn by the Banner Realty sign on

the coast road," Betty said, frowning. "You planning a trip out there?"

Rourke shrugged as he tucked the bag of batteries into his jacket pocket, then said goodbye to everyone in the store. He'd been anxious to get out of town before the storm struck, but his mind was suddenly focused on Annie Macintosh. While neighbors were helping neighbors prepare for the high winds and rain, boarding up windows and fueling generators, who was there to look out for her? Did she have any friends on the island at all?

The least he could do before he left was check on her. He could afford to stick around for a few more hours, maybe help her batten things down. The storm wasn't supposed to hit the coast until midnight and it was just past three in the afternoon.

He made a few more quick stops, for gas and snacks, then headed out along the coast. He made the turn at the sign and as he drove the winding road, he caught sight of the lighthouse. Rourke pulled the SUV to a stop, reconsidering what he was about to do.

Was this another one of those moments? Rourke wondered. Was this really about being a good neighbor, or was this about the strange attraction he felt for Annie Macintosh? An uneasy feeling came over him and he thought about turning the car around and heading back to the coast road.

After all, he was no white knight ready to ride to her rescue. "Come on, Buddy, give me a sign," he murmured.

A few seconds later, a sparrow, buffeted by the winds, landed on the hood of Rourke's car. The bird stared at him through the windshield. Rourke held his breath and a moment later, it flew off.

He cursed softly, then continued his drive toward the water. So many years had passed since they'd last seen each other. Did she really remember him or had he only imagined the look of recognition in her eyes?

The road was rutted and hard to navigate, his Range Rover bumping along as he tried to make out two tire tracks in front of him. When the light keeper's house finally came into view, he stopped the truck and stared out at the landscape.

The cottage had seen better days. The porch was sagging at one end, the chimney looked as if it was listing and the shutters that used to protect the house from storms like the one rolling in were falling off their hinges.

When he reached the house, Rourke turned off the ignition and hopped out of the truck. "Hello!" he shouted.

A dog barked in the distance and he walked up to the front door, avoiding the rotten step just in time. Rourke rapped on the door and waited. "Hello! Miss Macintosh?" A few seconds later, a border collie came charging around the corner of the house and Rourke froze, wondering if he'd be able to make it back to the truck before being bitten.

But the dog stopped short, then spun around and ran in the opposite direction. It stopped again, as if waiting for Rourke to follow him. He charged again and this time, Rourke held out his hand. The dog gave him a wary look as he came closer, then nudged Rourke's palm with his nose.

"Do you know where she is?" he asked.

The dog took off and Rourke followed, heading down a narrow path toward the sea. The lighthouse and keeper's cottage were set on land that had been scrubbed almost bare by the wind. The trees had been cleared long ago, leaving nothing to serve as a shield between the buildings and the white-capped Atlantic.

The surf was already high, the water roiling ahead of the storm blowing in from offshore. As he stared out at the horizon, he caught sight of Annie, standing on a small spit of sand and rock, the waves crashing around her and sending up huge plumes of water.

She was already wet, yet she didn't seem to notice. She just stared out at the slate-gray water, her eyes fixed on some distant point. The wind whipped her hair around her face and the roar was so loud that he doubted she'd be able to hear him.

The dog stood on the shore, barking at her, but she didn't turn around.

Another wave broke against the rocks and he watched as she struggled to keep her balance on her precarious perch. "What the hell are you doing?" he muttered. Rourke ran toward the shore, cupping his hands over his mouth and shouting at her to come back in.

To his relief, she turned at the sound of his voice. But at that exact moment, a rogue wave hit the rocks, slamming against her back and knocking her down. From where he was, Rourke couldn't see if she'd slid into the surf. He said a silent prayer that the water hadn't washed her away.

He made it down to the water in a matter of seconds, then climbed through the rocks. Rourke kept his eye on a small patch of maroon, the color of her jacket. When he reached her, she was lying on her back, the water rushing around her. Her eyes were closed and he leaned close, listening for her breathing. Rourke saw her chest move, then picked her up in his arms.

When they reached the safety of the shore, he laid her down in the tall grass and examined her for injuries. To his dismay, he found a cut on the back of her head that was bleeding into her wet hair. The dog circled around them both, whining and pawing at his mistress.

She moaned softly and her eyes fluttered open.

For a long moment, she stared up at him. And then a soft groan slipped from her lips and she closed her eyes again.

Rourke scooped up her limp body and tried as best as he could to carry her gently to the house. When he reached the back porch, he kicked the door in with his foot and it easily gave way.

The huge kitchen had been turned into a single living space. A stone fireplace dominated one wall of the kitchen and pulled up near it was a tattered easy chair and a small table with an oil lamp. An iron bed was nestled into a corner near the hearth and a well-worn braided rug covered the plank floor.

Rourke set her down on the bed, then leaned over her and rubbed her hands between his. God, even in this state, she was beautiful. Her lips were a perfect Cupid's bow and her skin was so flawless and smooth that he found himself reaching out to touch her.

As his fingertips made contact, she opened her eyes and looked up at him. "What are you doing here?" she murmured.

The stammer was gone and the sound of her voice sent a shiver through his body. He'd made a mistake in coming, Rourke thought to himself. The moment she spoke, he felt his world shift and he sensed that nothing would ever be the same again.

ANNIE'S HEAD ACHED and she was so cold she couldn't think clearly. Reaching back, she touched a sore spot on the crown of her head, then looked down at her fingers. "I'm bleeding."

"You hit your head on the rocks." He walked over to the sink and grabbed a dish towel, then returned and pressed it gently against her head. "Hold that."

She pinched her eyes shut, then opened them again. He was still there. He wasn't just a dream or a residual memory from earlier. He was sitting on the edge of the bed, staring at her, his handsome face etched with concern. She felt a shiver race through her. Her teeth chattered and her body trembled.

"Are you dizzy? Is your vision blurry? Do you feel nauseated?"

She stared at him, then shook her head. "No, I don't think so."

"I'm going to help you get out of those wet clothes. Do you have something warm to put on?"

Annie pointed to a fleece hoodie and a pair of flannel pajama bottoms tossed over the foot of the iron bed.

He gently turned her around and grabbed the collar of her jacket. Closing her eyes, she shrugged out of the jacket. Suddenly, she did feel a bit lightheaded. And when he reached for the bottom of her T-shirt, her heart began to race.

She drew a deep breath, then raised her arms over her head. She was naked beneath the T-shirt and the moment the cold air hit her damp skin, she crossed her arms over her breasts.

He handed her the hoodie and she slipped it on and zipped it up to her chin. Annie slowly turned and met his eyes. Though he tried to appear indifferent, she saw a flicker of desire there. His gaze fell to her mouth and for a moment, she thought he might kiss her. Then, he suddenly stood up.

"I'll let you take care of the rest," he murmured. "I'm going to go fetch some wood for the fire."

"There's no need," Annie said. "You don't have to stay. I'll be fine now."

"It's all right," he said. "It's no bother." He pointed to her head. "Keep pressure on that cut."

Annie nodded. It was odd for a virtual stranger to just walk into her house and start ordering her around. It was even odder that she was allowing it. "How did I get here?"

"I carried you," he said. "Your dog led me down to the water. What were you doing out there? You know how dangerous the waves can be before a storm." He shivered violently. "Is it always so cold in here?"

"There's no central heat. Just the wood-burning stove and the fireplace," she said.

As he opened the door, a chilly wind swirled

through the kitchen. "Rourke," she called. "Your name is Rourke, isn't it?"

He turned and smiled. "Rourke Quinn." With that, he walked outside.

Annie sat up and swung her legs off the bed. Her head hurt, but she wasn't dizzy or confused. Well, maybe a little, but that was more from having a handsome man in her house than the wound on her head. She slipped off her shoes and socks. Standing beside the bed, she gingerly skimmed the wet jeans down over her hips and kicked them aside.

Shivering, she grabbed the pajama bottoms and tugged them on, then crawled beneath the faded handmade quilts on the bed. Drawing a deep breath, she closed her eyes. She led a rather lonely existence, but she'd never really regretted her choice of a simple life—until now.

This was the only home she'd ever known. After her parents passed away, her grandmother had taken her in. From that moment on, her life had changed. She'd been allowed to roam free, without any rules or expectations. She ate when she was hungry, slept when she was tired and in between, explored every inch of the land that surrounded her home.

For a young girl who struggled to communicate, it was the perfect life. Her friends were wild animals and sea creatures, clouds and trees, the wonderful, vibrant natural world waiting just outside the door of the light keeper's cottage. They didn't care whether her words came out in fits and starts. She lived her life in her fantasies, where she had friends, where people thought she was beautiful and clever, and where her stammer didn't exist.

It was odd. Annie had imagined that someone would someday rescue her from her lonely existence. And her white knight had always looked exactly like Rourke Quinn. From the moment he'd defended her against the town bullies, he'd become her hero. And now, here he was, coming to her rescue again. Only she wasn't a child anymore. She was a twenty-five-year-old woman.

Over the years, her fantasies had given way to a simple reality. She was alone and no one was coming to ease her loneliness. So she'd accepted her life as it was and learned to be happy.

Maybe it seemed strange to others on the island, but it was a life she'd come to enjoy, even love. She had her paintings and her poetry and plenty of time for her own thoughts. Still, she couldn't deny that she was grateful for the company, especially with the approaching storm.

It wasn't just because he was handsome or sexy or even a tiny bit dangerous. Annie had weathered storms in the past and they'd always left her shaken, filled with bad memories of her parents' deaths. Perhaps if she had someone with her during the worst of it, it wouldn't be so traumatic.

The door flew open and Rourke stepped back inside, his arms loaded with firewood. He strode to the hearth and carefully stacked the wood on the stone apron. Then, he tossed a few birch logs onto the flickering embers. A moment later, flames licked at the white bark.

He sat back on his heels and stared into the fire. "How do you feel?" he asked.

"Better," she said. "Thank you. For rescuing me."

He turned to look at her and she took in the details of his face. There was something so kind about his eyes, even set in an expression that seemed less than happy. "You should go. You don't want to be caught out here when the storm rolls in."

"I have some tools in my truck," he said. "The wind is supposed to be bad. I'm going to get your shutters squared away and then I'll leave."

"You don't have to—"

"No, I'm not sure I could leave you here without making this place a little safer."

"It's held up to almost a hundred years of storms. I'm sure it will hold up to one more," Annie said.

"I'm not so sure," Rourke replied. "This is supposed to be a bad one."

Annie shrugged. "I can't stop it from coming, so worrying about the wind never did much good. Whatever will happen, will happen."

He gave her an odd look. "How is your head? Are you confused?"

Annie pulled the towel away. "I think it's stopped bleeding."

"Just stay put," he said. "Lie down and rest. Do you want me to light the stove? I could make you a cup of tea."

"No, I'll be fine." She paused. "Why are you doing this, Rourke Quinn?"

"Because no one else seems to be worried about you," he said. He went to the door and stepped outside.

How long had it been since she'd thought about him? When had she let go of that fantasy? Annie hadn't realized how much she'd missed him—and her fantasies—until now. But something had changed. Her fantasies were now much more—erotic.

She sank back into the down pillows and stared up at the ceiling, smiling to herself. Now that she had him here, what would she do with him?

She hadn't been completely isolated over the years. There had been men who wandered in and out of her life, usually in the summer months when the population of the island swelled from the tourists. There had been a fellow artist a few years back who had come to paint her lighthouse and ended up staying until the first frost. And then the guy from the coast guard who came to check the light every three months. They'd occasionally indulged in a night of pleasure after a few glasses of wine.

What would it take to get Rourke to stay for the night? Would he be so easy to seduce? Annie groaned softly. She'd come to the realization that most single men were quite willing to indulge, especially when there were no strings attached. But not all of them understood her rather unconventional thoughts about sex.

So yes, she'd lived a very simple life since she was a child. Left without a means of support, she'd managed to eke out an existence in a house that had no phone, no electricity and very crude plumbing. She didn't own a television or a computer.

Annie understood exactly what was necessary to sustain life. She ate a simple and natural diet, supplemented occasionally with fish or crab or oysters she gathered herself, and eggs from a local farmer. Her clothes weren't purchased for beauty but for functionality and durability. And her men, well, they were chosen to satisfy a very natural and powerful need. Like everything else in her life, sex, and the intimacy it brought, was essential to her existence. Like water…or oxygen…or warmth.

Reaching for the book on her bedside table,

Annie tried to distract herself by reading. But it was impossible to think about anything but Rourke. She listened as he moved from window to window, closing the shutters and then fastening them with screws. As the last of the natural light disappeared, she crawled from the bed and began to light the kerosene lamps scattered around the room.

He left the two windows on the porch uncovered, probably choosing to wait until the wind got worse. Then she heard his truck start. Frowning, Annie crawled out of bed and hurried to the door, wondering if he'd chosen to leave after all. But just as she reached the door, it swung open again, nearly hitting her in the face. Kit, her dog, slipped in ahead of him.

"What are you doing out of bed?" he asked, raking his hands through his windblown hair.

"I—I thought you were leaving. I wanted to say goodbye. And to thank you."

"I'm not going anywhere," he said. "I just moved my truck closer to the cottage. What else do you need?"

"I'm fine," she said.

He stared at her for a long moment. When he finally looked away, Annie felt the butterflies in her stomach intensify. It was clear he was attracted to her. He wasn't even trying to hide it.

"Tea," he said. "I'll make some tea." He shrugged

out of his jacket and then moved to the sink. She watched as he glanced around, looking for the water faucet.

"You have to pump it," she said. "There is no indoor plumbing."

"No indoor—" He turned to face her. "You don't have a shower? Or a toilet?"

"Sure. But they run on a rainwater catch system. I put it in about five years ago. There's a shower in the lighthouse with a water heater. But here in the house, there's just a bath, with water from the hand pump heated on the stove."

"There's no electricity either?"

Annie shook her head. "I don't really need it. There's nothing I need to run."

"No television? No computer?"

"I have a phone. I recharge that in the lighthouse. There's a little refrigerator out there, too, but I rarely use it. It's really not that unusual. A lot of people live this way."

"For this day and age it is," he said. "Where do you get the firewood?"

"Sam Decker brings it around," she said. "Except for food and taxes, it's my only expense."

Sam Decker had been one of the bullies who had taunted her as a child, making fun of her stammer by doing a dead-on imitation of her. But he'd come to regret his actions and one day, after her grandmother had passed away, he'd shown up on her front porch with a cord of split wood and an apology.

Since then, he'd brought wood every month and helped her with little jobs around the house. Though they were both adults now, and they were able to be cordial, even friendly, the wounds ran deep. She'd outgrown her stammer, but she still couldn't fully trust Sam. And so she kept him at arm's length.

Annie knew Sam had romantic feelings for her and hoped for something more than just friendship. But there was absolutely no attraction on her end. When there was attraction, she couldn't deny it… like now…with Rourke.

She watched as he built a fire in the stove, studying his backside, clad in faded denim. He added small pieces of kindling from the basket beneath the sink and when the flames were high enough, he dropped a log on top of the fire. Rourke closed the cast-iron door, then worked to fill the battered kettle with water from the pump.

Annie walked over to the cabinets above the sink. She pulled back the gingham fabric and revealed two jars of loose tea. "I have black or green. Which do you prefer?"

"Black," he said.

She retrieved an old china teapot from the breakfront and set it on the stove, then scooped a measure of the tea into it. After that, she found a pair of mugs and set them beside the pot. "I don't have real cream. Or milk. Just powdered milk," she said.

"Just a little sugar would be good," he said.

ROURKE WASN'T QUITE sure what to think about all of this. Of course, he'd known there were people in the world who lived without the trappings of technology. He'd never actually met one, though. And a single woman living alone seemed like an unlikely candidate for pioneer of the year.

"What are you thinking?" she asked, watching him with an inquisitive expression.

"I'm just…I don't know. Surprised. Maybe a little confused."

"About how I live?"

He nodded. "That…among other things."

"I didn't really choose this life," she said. "I guess it chose me—out of necessity. I don't have a lot of money, so I have to be careful what I spend. You'd be surprised at how little you can live on when you simplify things."

"I can imagine," he said.

"I think everyone should at least try to reduce the impact they have on our environment. It's just healthier. For me and the planet."

"What about a car?"

"I don't have one. I bike into town. In the winter, I walk. It's only three miles. It's good exercise."

He'd never known anyone quite like her. And Rourke had known a lot of women. Though he'd admired beauty and wit in the opposite sex, there had always been something he found lacking in his female companions. But here was a woman who was strong and independent. She had courage and determination and a quiet confidence that he found endlessly attractive.

He was curious about her life. How had she transformed herself from that painfully shy girl with the stutter into a strong, capable woman? "You remembered my name," he said.

Annie nodded. "You were kind to me once."

"You've changed. A lot."

"I've grown up." She paused. "You probably mean the stammer? That disappeared after I got out of school. I didn't want to live my life in a constant state of fear and I reached a point where I just stopped fighting. I didn't feel it necessary to defend myself anymore. I found an inner calm and I think my mind caught up with my words."

"You seem happy," Rourke said.

"I am."

"But you don't have many friends on the island."

"I don't need a lot of friends. Those that I have are good to me. Besides, how many true friends do we really have? Most people in your life are acquaintances not friends. How many would come to you if you called?"

He shrugged. She was right. He didn't have that many good friends. He could count them on one hand. The whistle from the teakettle shattered the silence between them and Rourke stood up and walked back to the stove. He poured the water into the pot.

"There's a strainer on the stove," she said.

He tossed the strainer into one of the mugs, then carried everything over to the hearth, carefully setting the china pot on the flat stone. "Don't you ever get lonely?"

"All the time," she said. "But there's really not much I can do about it. Leaving the island would be like cutting out a part of my heart."

"Have you *ever* left the island?" he asked.

This brought a laugh. "Of course I have. All the time."

He could see it in her eyes. She was lying. But now was not the time to call her on it. "I live in New York," he said.

"Good for you. When I imagine living my life there, it seems as difficult to me as my life here seems to you."

A gust of wind rattled the windows and they both turned to look. "It's going to get a lot worse before it gets better."

Annie crawled out of her chair and sat down

next to him on the hearth. Rourke felt his pulse quicken and he held tight to his tea in an effort not to reach out and touch her. But she had other ideas. She set her mug down and reached out, placing her hand on his cheek. Then, her gaze fixed on his, she leaned forward and touched her lips to his.

The contact sent a jolt running through him, like being struck by lightning. Only it wasn't painful, but warm and pleasurable. He set his mug down beside him and slipped his fingers through her hair, pulling her into another kiss, this one deeper and more urgent than the first.

Rourke wasn't sure what was happening, but he wasn't about to stop it. From the moment he'd seen her in the hardware store, he'd wanted this to happen. He'd just never expected to get the chance. And now that he was here, Rourke wasn't going to waste another moment.

His fingers twisted in the damp strands of her hair, but suddenly he heard her gasp and Rourke drew back. He'd forgotten about the cut on her scalp. "Let me look," he said.

"It's really much better," she said. "It just stings a little."

The interior of the cabin was dimly lit, the sun already down and the lamps providing a feeble kind of light. He gently examined her injury by the glow of the fire and found the spot. There was a substantial knot around the cut, but it looked as if it had stopped bleeding.

"I don't think it will need stitches."

"Good," she said. "I hate going to the doctor."

"What the hell were you doing out there?" Rourke asked. "You've lived by the ocean your entire life. Surely you know better than anyone how dangerous it can be." He paused. "And what was the herring for? Who buys twenty pounds of bait before a storm?"

"Are you hungry? I should make us something for dinner."

"You didn't answer my question," he asked. "What were you doing?"

"Talking to the sea," she said. "When it gets like this, sometimes I think I can hear voices in the wind. If I just listen hard enough, I think I might be able to hear what they're saying."

"Voices? Whose voices?"

"My parents'," she said softly. He saw a blush rise on her cheeks. "It's silly. I know."

Rourke said, "No, it's not. It's not." He wanted to ask her what had happened. Town gossip had never gone into great detail. He knew they'd both drowned, but he wasn't sure of the circumstances. No one in town had ever offered an explanation and until now, it really hadn't mattered to him.

"I really should stop. This time it almost got me killed."

"I guess you were lucky I was there," he said.

She nodded. "I guess I was." Annie tucked her feet up beneath her and wrapped her arms around her legs. "Are you sure you don't have someplace you need to be?"

"Actually, I was on my way home to New York. I was hoping to put a few miles behind me before the storm hit. But I can stay."

"Maybe you should bring your things in before the weather gets too bad. I'll just get dinner started."

Rourke nodded. He stood, grabbed his jacket and slipped into it. "What's the dog's name?"

"Kit," she said.

Rourke patted his thigh and the dog looked up from where he was sleeping by the fire. "Come on, boy."

The border collie jumped to his feet and scampered to the door, then hurried out in front of Rourke. As he walked down the steps, he noticed that the wind had picked up and the temperature had dropped close to freezing. If it got any colder, the rain might become ice or snow.

He moved toward the water. The color of the sky and sea now blended together until the horizon was almost impossible to see. The wind gusts were strong enough to test his balance and within minutes, his fingers had gone numb from the cold.

Kit stood beside him, sniffing at the wind.

Rourke reached down and gave him a pat on the head. She wasn't entirely alone, he mused. And maybe she would have been fine without his help. But Rourke couldn't regret his impulse to stop and check on her.

After all, she'd kissed him. And he hadn't been kissed—or touched—by a woman since he'd arrived on the island. It was rather ironic that all this was happening the day he decided to head home. He wasn't going to question the timing. Whatever happened tonight between them could be a powerful counterpoint to the storm.

2

"CAN YOU PEEL potatoes?" Annie glanced over her shoulder at Rourke. He sat at the kitchen table, watching her move about the kitchen as she prepared dinner. "I think I can manage," he said. "Unless you're going to make me do it with a knife."

"I do have a vegetable peeler." She reached into a wicker basket on the shelf above the sink and grabbed it, then placed some potatoes in a bowl.

"I wasn't sure you had one of these newfangled things," he said, holding up the peeler.

"I'm glad you find my life so amusing."

Rourke picked up a potato. "Not amusing. Endlessly fascinating." His gaze met hers and Annie felt a shiver skitter down her spine. The longer they were cooped up in this cottage, the harder it was to deny the attraction between them. It was like waiting for the storm to hit. She wasn't sure when it was going to happen, but it would happen. And when it did it would be powerful and impossible to ignore.

"I like being self-sufficient," she said. "I like not having to depend on anyone."

"Someone brings you wood."

"I could get my own wood," she said. "It would just take so much time out of my day that it wouldn't be worth it. But I could do it."

"I'm sure you could," Rourke said. "I suspect you could do just about anything you set your mind to."

She grabbed a small bunch of carrots she'd brought up from the root cellar and sat down, placing them on the table. Cupping her chin in her hand, she observed him as he peeled the potatoes. Annie was used to doing things her own way, so she fought the urge to give him advice.

"It's going to be a long night," she murmured.

Rourke glanced up. "Are you worried?"

She shook her head. Storms usually put her on edge, but Annie felt remarkably calm. Rourke was a wonderful distraction. "I like having you here. I'm glad you stayed."

"Is that why you kissed me?" he asked.

Annie wondered when the subject of their kiss would come up. She couldn't help but smile. "I'm not sure why I did that."

"Oh, come on," Rourke said. "I know enough

about you already to know that you never do anything without a reason. So tell me, Annie. Why did you kiss me?"

He was right. She was the least impulsive person on all of Cape Breton Island. "I wanted to let you know I was…interested. And what about you? Are you interested?"

"Interested in kissing you again? The answer to that would be yes. I'm very interested."

"I think we should try it again," Annie said.

"Now? Because, I think now would be as good a time as any."

"All right," she said. They stared at each other across the table. "Are you going to come to me or am I going to come to you?"

"I think you should come to me," Rourke suggested.

Annie wiped her damp hands on a dish towel, then slowly stood. As she circled the table, her heart began to race and she felt as if her knees would buckle. When she stood in front of him, she reached out to smooth her hand through his thick, dark hair. But he caught her fingers and opened her hand, pressing his lips to the center of her palm.

She watched as he slipped his hands around her waist and gently drew her closer. Nuzzling his face against her belly, Rourke drew a long, deep breath. When he looked up at her again, Annie could see that they weren't going to stop at just one kiss.

Furrowing her fingers through his hair, she tipped his face up. Slowly, she sank down until their mouths were nearly touching. His breath was warm on her lips, but she waited, resisting the urge to surrender. But Rourke wasn't nearly so determined. With a low moan, he yanked her into a kiss, pulling her into his lap at the same time.

The depth of his passion startled her at first. It felt as if they'd skipped a few steps along the way. But Annie wasn't going to fight him. This was exactly what she was hoping would happen. They had the whole night ahead of them and this was a promising beginning to it all.

His kiss was determined, almost desperate, searching for the perfect melding of their mouths. His fingers twisted through the hair at her nape and when he finally drew back, his breath came in short gasps. He moved to kiss her again, but Kit suddenly jumped up from his spot next to the fire and began to bark at the door.

A few moments later, a knock sounded. Annie glanced down at him. "Are you expecting company?" he asked.

"I don't think so," she said. She ran her fingers through her hair as she walked to the door. When she pulled it open, a gust of wind nearly tore it from her hands. A tall, slender figure stepped inside and when he pushed his hood away from his face, she recognized Sam Decker. He was still dressed in his uniform from his job as a regional police officer and Annie wasn't sure if the visit was personal or professional.

Sam quickly took his cap off and smiled at her. "Hey, it's getting nasty out there."

"Hi, Sam," she murmured.

He started to shrug out of his jacket before he noticed Rourke sitting across the room. He frowned, then glanced back and forth between the two of them. "Quinn. I heard you were on your way off the island." He cleared his throat. "What are you doing here?"

"I just stopped by to check on Annie," Rourke said. "What about you?"

"Same. I just wanted to check…to make sure she had enough wood to get her through the storm."

"You brought wood just last week," Annie interrupted.

"We're fine here," Rourke said. "We have everything we need, right, Annie?"

"I didn't realize you two were…friends," Sam said.

Annie nodded. "We've known each other since we were kids," she said.

Sam shrugged. "Is your cell phone charged?"

Annie nodded and took his arm, leading him back to the door. "If I need any help, I'll be sure to call."

Sam nodded reluctantly. "All right, then. I'm on duty tonight and my advice is to stay inside. If there's trouble, dial 911."

She opened the door and let him out, then closed it behind her, leaning against the scarred wood. Rourke slowly stood and crossed the room. He reached out and tucked a strand of hair behind her ear.

"Are you sure you wanted him to leave?" he murmured, leaning close.

"Yes," Annie replied, her pulse quickening. She'd done this before, but it had never felt quite so dangerous. There were feelings here, emotions that she couldn't quite describe. She felt vulnerable and out of control, but Annie couldn't seem to stop herself from wanting him.

"When was the last time you kissed him?" Rourke murmured.

"Who?"

"Sam Decker."

"I've never kissed Sam," she said.

"He wants to kiss you," Rourke said. "It's written all over his face."

"He has too many expectations."

"Expectations?"

"He thinks he wants to take care of me. He wants to marry me. But I'm not looking for anything like that."

"You just like having sex with strangers?"

"Not strangers. I prefer…uncomplicated men."

"Is that what I am, Annie?"

"You were on your way home. And I expect you will be again once the storm passes. That makes things between us very simple."

"So you're just using me for sex?"

Annie laughed. "That's putting it rather bluntly."

"I think we ought to be clear about our intentions, don't you?"

It sounded as if the notion of no-strings sex was insulting to him. But then, maybe he was just teasing her. Or maybe he wanted to be sure of her motives. "No expectations," she said.

"All right. But if you expect me to jump into bed with you, you could at least give me dinner first."

Annie smiled. "All right. I do have a bottle of wine we could share." She moved to a cabinet near the sink and pulled a bottle of Merlot out. When she found the corkscrew, she opened the wine and poured it into two mismatched jelly jars. "I don't have proper wineglasses. These are recycled."

He raised the jelly glass. "To the storm that brought us together," he said.

Annie touched her glass to his. "The storm."

As she sipped her wine and cut vegetables for the lentil stew, Annie listened to the wind howl outside and the shutters rattle. The anticipation was almost too much to bear. In her mind she was already undressing him and pulling his naked body onto the bed with her. She couldn't remember ever wanting a man as much as she wanted him.

They'd have one night together. But would that be enough? Or would she be left wanting more?

BY THE TIME dinner was over, they'd gone through Annie's bottle of wine. She'd offered him whiskey, but Rourke already felt the effects of the wine and he wanted to keep his wits about him.

It had taken every ounce of his willpower not to drag her off to the comfortable bed tucked into the corner near the hearth. They both knew what they wanted, but for some reason, Annie had chosen to prolong his agony.

After finishing the dishes, she'd grabbed a book and curled up in the overstuffed chair near the fire, an oil lamp providing scant light to read by. Rourke was left to pace the cabin, peering out the window of the kitchen door and wondering why she was delaying the inevitable.

Every twenty seconds, a beam from the lighthouse swept across the sky, illuminating the wind-driven rain and the bent trees. "The rain is turning to sleet," he murmured.

She glanced up from her book. "Hmm. It's gotten colder."

"Are you cold? I can put more wood on the fire."

"There comes a point when it doesn't do any

good. The fire can't keep up with the dropping temperatures."

"What do you do then?"

"Crawl beneath the covers and pull them up over my head."

He stared at her for a long moment. Was she suggesting it was time to go to bed? And was she inviting him to crawl in beside her?

Annie seemed completely unconcerned about the weather. Rourke wanted to know the details of the storm, how long it would last, how much rain they'd get, whether the waves were breaking over the Canso Causeway yet. If he were at his uncle's place, he'd turn on the Weather Network and all his questions would be answered. "You said you had a radio?"

She nodded.

"I think I'm going to see if I can find a weather report."

Annie shook her head. "The batteries are dead," she said. "I forgot to get some new ones."

"I have batteries. I bought them at the hardware store earlier."

She sighed. "I'm not sure where it is," Annie said. "It's just an old transistor."

"Don't you think it might be good to know what's going on out there?"

"Listening to the radio isn't going to make the storm go away," she said. "When it's done, it's done. It will stop raining and the wind will stop blowing and everything will get back to normal. If you want to know what the storm is doing, then you should go outside and see for yourself."

"You're crazy," he said.

Annie closed the book and got to her feet. "Come on. I'll show you. I do it all the time."

She slipped her bare feet into a pair of wellies, then pulled her slicker off the hook near the door. "It's freezing out there. Put that cap on. And don't forget your gloves."

"We don't need to go outside," he insisted.

"I want to see how high the storm surge is." Annie picked up a lantern from the table near the door, lit it, then stepped outside. Rourke frowned. There was absolutely no telling her what to do. For some odd reason, he found that one of her most endearing qualities.

Rourke quickly pulled on his jacket. He found her waiting for him on the porch. Annie held out her hand and they stepped into the midst of the storm.

The strong wind made it hard to stand upright, but they both leaned into it. Sleet stung his cheeks and he could barely see a few feet in front of him, even with the flickering lantern. But he knew, without a doubt, that he'd never forget this experience.

Kit danced around their feet, then ran off into

the darkness, barking. He could smell the sea in the air and could hear the crash of the waves on the rocks. It seemed that every sense in his body had become sharply attuned.

They stopped near the shore and stared out at the horizon. With each pass of the light, they could see the angry water, the spray of the waves and the flood of water reaching farther onto the shore. The house was set at least thirty feet higher than the sea and safe from the worst surge.

"You're right," he shouted.

She looked over at him. He could see that she was mouthing a word, then realized it was impossible to hear each other in the roar of the storm. Instead, he slipped his arm around her waist and pulled her against him. His lips came down on hers, cold and damp. But as she opened to his kiss, a wonderful warmth flooded through his bloodstream. The wind buffeted them, threatening to knock them off their feet, but he held tight to her as the kiss intensified.

When he finally drew back, he could barely see her face. He reached down and ran his thumb over her cold cheek, cupping her face in his hands. "I think we should go inside," he shouted.

"Come with me," she replied. Annie grabbed his hand and drew him deeper into the storm. They ran toward the lighthouse, the beam of light guiding the way. When they reached the door, she pulled a key from her jacket pocket and unlocked it. They stumbled inside, Kit scampering in, too, and shut the door behind them.

A moment later, Rourke heard a switch flip and the interior was flooded in light. He stared at the spacious room, a circular iron stair dominating the center. Like most of the lighthouses on Cape Breton, this was a pyramidal-shaped tower that narrowed as it got taller. Annie walked over to a small painted table and set the lantern down. She grabbed her cell phone, holding it up to him as she unplugged it. "Charged," she said.

The room was quite cozy, with antique furniture scattered around the perimeter. "Bathroom is through that door," she said. "If you want to take a hot shower, you have to turn on the water heater and wait about an hour."

"I don't need a shower," he said. "At least not now."

Rourke wandered over to the table and examined the old radio sitting on top of it. He flipped it on and found it turned to a station playing Celtic music. The strains of fiddle and mandolin echoed upward.

The wind howled outside and the old wooden structure creaked with each gust. "I'm going to go up and watch the storm," she said. Rourke watched as she climbed the stairs. Her skin was flawless, pale, marked only by a light dusting of freckles across her nose. Her auburn hair curled gently around her face and shoulders. And that body. Had no one here ever noticed how beautiful she was?

Everything about her was made for a man's touch. Most of the women in New York City worked out two hours a day to get a body like Annie's. She was lithe and fit, not from spending time in a gym, but because she lived a simple life.

She needed so little to be happy—a roof over her head, a warm fire, a good book. And she needed him, at least for the night. He closed his eyes and wondered at the fates that brought him here.

Had he followed his original plan, he'd be back on the mainland by now, headed toward the border and Bangor, Maine. He'd intended to stop there for the night, but now, he'd be spending the night in Annie's bed.

It felt right. Though they didn't really know each other in the traditional sense, there was a connection. He felt it every time he touched her… and kissed her. Maybe this had all been part of some cosmic plan—their encounter at the hardware store, the coming storm and the memories that flooded his mind upon seeing her.

He opened his eyes, then crossed the room to the circular stairs. He crawled upward to the top, into the darkness, and when he reached the platform, he found her standing near the window, her hands pressed against the thick glass.

The light was so blinding that he had to squint every time it made a rotation. He stepped up behind her and wrapped his arms around her waist. Annie leaned into his body.

"My mother died on a night just like this," she murmured. "They found her body the next morning, on the rocks."

"What happened?"

Annie shrugged. "She was sad. Depressed. Suicidal. She'd always been troubled, but my father thought he could fix her. That's why he brought her here to live. Away from the city. Away from temptation. But she was so miserable here."

"I'm sorry," he said.

"He blamed himself. He used to row out into the cove in the middle of the night. He said he could hear her, he could talk to her. They found his boat right over there," she said, pointing. "They never found him. We buried an empty coffin next to her in the cemetery."

Rourke slowly turned her toward him. "You've had a lot of loss in your life."

Annie nodded, reaching up to touch his face. "Make love to me."

"Here?"

"Anywhere," she said. "I don't care. I need to get these thoughts out of my head."

He took her hand and led her to the top of the stairs. "Let's go back to the house."

THEY RAN BACK through the storm, Annie breathless with anticipation and a bit of trepidation. If she were listening to her instincts, this would not be happening. She'd always maintained a careful distance in her physical encounters with men. But the only thing she could think about with Rourke was getting as close to him as possible.

The moment they stepped inside the house, Annie reached for the zipper on her slicker. But he grabbed her hands and warmed them between his, slowly drawing her toward the fire.

She could hear her heart beating, could feel the pulse in her veins. Every physical sensation seemed more acute, and when Rourke slowly began to remove her clothes, she grasped his shoulder, afraid that her knees might buckle beneath her. First her gloves, then her slicker, Rourke tossing both on the floor.

Annie didn't want to wait any longer. The storm inside her body was raging out of control and the only way to quell it was Rourke's touch on her naked body. But he would not be deterred. When she reached for the hem of her hoodie, he grabbed her hand. "Slow down," he said, brushing his lips against hers. "Let me get the fire going."

"The only place we'll be warm is in bed," she

said. Annie pulled the hoodie over her head. The cold air prickled her skin into goose bumps and brought her nipples to hard peaks.

Rourke's breath caught as his gaze drifted down to her naked breasts. "My hands are cold," he said, his fingers skimming around her waist.

"Put some wood on the fire," she said. Annie kicked off her wellies, then walked over to the bed. Turning her back to him, she pulled her jeans off. A shiver skittered through her body and she pulled the covers back and slipped between the faded sheets.

Rourke stood over the hearth, his gaze fixed on the crackling fire. Kit had already curled up in front of the hearth, grateful for the warmth.

"Come to bed," Annie said.

Rourke turned to her and smiled. "Are you sure you want to do this?"

She'd never wanted anything more in her life. The ache to have him beside her, inside her, ran deep. She could feel it, and the only way to stop it was mind-numbing passion and unbridled desire.

Annie watched as he slowly undressed in front of her. He didn't seem to be bothered that she stared, taking in every detail of his beautiful body. She'd been with a number of men, but never with anyone quite so physically perfect. He was slender but muscular, wide shoulders and narrow hips.

His damp hair clung to his neck and he shook

his head, sending droplets across the quilt. Annie threw the covers back, a silent invitation.

"Is this how they did it in the olden days?"

"Did what?"

"Kept warm."

Annie nodded. "You'll like it. I promise."

His gaze took in her naked body, moving from shoulder to hip. "I already do."

Rourke rummaged through his leather duffel and pulled out a box of condoms, unopened. "We may need these," he said before he crawled in beside her.

She took the box and smiled. "You came prepared?"

"I bought that in New York," Rourke replied. "It's been a while." He laid beside her, finding her hand and drawing it up to his lips. "I'm glad I decided to stay."

"Me, too. I'm usually alone during these storms. I can never sleep."

"The wind?"

"The dreams," she said.

"Then I'll just have to distract your thoughts and keep you warm." He chuckled softly. "How to do that?" Slipping his hand beneath the covers, Rourke wrapped his arm around her waist, then pulled her body against his. She felt a flood of desire course through her body and Annie felt the last of her doubts crumble beneath his touch.

"Kiss me," she murmured, her gaze searching his. "That would be a good start." Her palm ran along his hip, then back up again. Just that simple teasing touch was enough to cause a groan to slip from his throat.

"I almost turned around," he whispered.

"Where?"

"Up the hill. Earlier this afternoon. But something was drawing me here and I couldn't stop myself. I needed to see you, to make sure you were all right."

"Why?"

Rourke shook his head. "I don't know. Did you recognize me in the hardware store?"

Annie nodded. "I did. I'd heard someone talking about you at the post office last month and I was hoping I'd see you."

"Really?"

"I wanted to see the kind of man you'd become. I needed to see that you were still someone kind and good. And you are. You came here to check on me. You pulled me off the rocks."

He bent close and kissed her. "I think I'm warming up," Rourke murmured.

Annie smiled. "I think so, too."

She reached between them and smoothed her fingertips along the length of his rigid shaft. Rourke's breath caught in his throat and he nuzzled his face into the curve of her neck, his breathing growing quick and shallow. Slowly, Annie began to stroke him in a long, slow rhythm.

When her caress became too much for him to bear, Rourke took control, pinning her hands above her head and rolling on top of her. Their mouths met in a long, lingering kiss. Annie writhed beneath him, his shaft pressed into her belly.

She didn't want to wait any longer, desperate to feel him moving inside of her. But Rourke was determined to keep her waiting. "Don't move," he warned. "Stay still."

Slowly, he kissed a path from her lips to her neck and then to her shoulder. Inch by inch, he moved lower, pausing at her breasts to tease each nipple with his tongue. Her fingers tangled in his damp hair and she gasped as he drew one nipple taut before doing the same to the other.

When he disappeared beneath the bedcovers, she didn't stop him and when he found the spot between her legs, she parted her thighs to give him access. She was damp with desire and when he tasted her, her body jerked in response. He teased her, bringing her close, then letting her fall back again. Annie sensed his purpose and she fought against her release, knowing that if she did, they could share their pleasure together.

By the time he relented, Annie was desperate, her body on the edge, her mind spinning with need. Rourke grabbed a condom from the package on the bedside table, fumbling with it. She took it from him and tore the package open. With a gentle touch, she deftly sheathed him.

Though she had waited patiently for this very moment, now that it had arrived, she wasn't sure she was ready. She wanted him too much, needed him as she'd never needed a man before. And she wasn't looking for just physical release. She wanted a deeper connection. She wanted to—

Annie bit her bottom lip, trying to banish the thought from her head. But it was there, burned into her brain. She wanted to feel what it might be like to be loved by a man. And not just any man, but by Rourke Quinn. He'd been her hero since she was a girl, her fantasy since she was a teen and now, he'd become her lover.

Annie pressed him back into the pillows and straddled his hips. Rourke smiled, as if enjoying the act of complete surrender. Slowly, deliciously, she sank onto his hard shaft, taking him deep inside her. Annie could tell that just that single thrust had rocked his self-control. He held tight to her hips until he could regain his composure.

But Annie didn't want to wait any longer. From the moment he'd walked in her front door, she'd known this was how it would be. The attraction was just too much to deny. She closed her eyes and tipped her head back, then slowly began to move.

She waited for the pleasure, for that slow, steady climb to her release. But it wasn't there.

Only when she opened her eyes and looked down at him could she find it. Their gazes locked and Annie could see his desire smoldering.

As her pace increased, he drew her into another kiss, then rolled her beneath him, capturing control again. Thrusting slowly and deeply, Annie felt her body respond and she knew he could bring her to the edge just one more time.

And when he did, he didn't bother to stop. Instead, he joined her in a sweet, intense surrender, driving into her until she dissolved into shudders and spasms of release. His own orgasm seemed to go on forever, and when he was finally spent, he drew back and looked down into her flushed face.

Annie smiled.

"What?" he asked.

"I've never had that fantasy before," she said, a shudder of satisfaction racing through her body.

"Fantasy?" Rourke asked, rolling off her to lie at her side. He pulled her naked body against his, throwing his leg over her thighs.

Annie nodded as she turned to face him, folding her hands beneath her cheek. "After you stood up for me that time with the bullies, you became my imaginary hero. I used to make up these wild stories in my head and you'd always show up at just the right time and save me. You were always part prince, part superhero."

"I think maybe you saved me," he said, brushing a strand of hair from her eyes. "Maybe I was supposed to stay on this island tonight."

"It might still be raining tomorrow," Annie said.

"Are you asking me to stay another night?"

"Maybe. Just one, that's all."

"I think that can be arranged," Rourke replied.

Considering how well their first night together had gone, Annie was looking forward to more of the same tomorrow night. In truth, she was secretly hoping the storm would last a week. But even then, that might not be enough time to diminish her need for him. Though she wasn't ready to admit it yet, there was a good chance that her need might never diminish.

3

ANNIE SNUGGLED BENEATH the covers, drawing the quilt up around her face to warm her cold nose. She reached out to search for the man who'd spent most of the night seducing her but Rourke's side of the bed was empty.

She pushed up on her elbow and looked around the room, then saw him peering out the window in the kitchen door, staring at the storm. He'd pulled on his jeans, but his upper body and feet were bare. "Is it still raining?" she asked.

"Yeah," he said. "It looks like everything is covered with ice out there.

Annie crawled out of bed, pulling the quilt around her naked body. She looked out into the morning light. The wind was still blowing and wisps of surf from the shore spun up into the air with each gust. "It's early for ice," she murmured. "I wonder if the power is out anywhere."

"I've never been here in early October." He turned and wrapped his arms around her waist. "Good thing I don't have to be anywhere today. Except here."

She shivered. "Come back to bed. It's too cold to be up."

"Let me put some wood on the fire," he said.

She glanced over at the hearth. "There is no more wood."

"I stacked some on the porch yesterday afternoon," he said. "I'll just grab some."

Annie watched him go outside. A few seconds later, he was back, shaking the cold off his bare feet, his chest shining with droplets of rain. Rourke crossed to the hearth and dumped the wood on the floor, then went out for another load.

After he'd brought in another armful, he threw a few logs on the embers. Annie held out her hand, then pulled him back onto the bed. "I guess we can stay in bed all day now," she said. "It's going to take me that long to warm you up."

"Darling, I guarantee it won't take you all day."

Annie laughed, then smoothed her palm down his belly, her fingertips dipping beneath the waistband of his jeans. His stomach growled softly and Rourke drew her hips against his. "I think you're going to need to feed me first," he said, nuzzling her neck. "I can't keep up with this pace if I don't have some nourishment."

"Crawl under the covers, then," she said. "I'll light the stove and make us some eggs."

"No, you stay in bed and I'll make breakfast for you."

He shrugged out of the blanket and wrapped it back around her. But Annie got out of bed and settled herself in the chair near the fire, tucking her feet beneath her.

She observed him silently as he searched out ingredients for breakfast. In the end, he settled on French toast, slicing the bread she'd made yesterday morning and dipping it into the fresh eggs Danny Phalen had dropped off the day before.

When it was ready, he brought it over, along with the butter dish and a tin of maple syrup, and set it on the hearth. He returned to the kitchen to pour two mugs of coffee from the percolator on the stove, then sat down across from her.

"This looks lovely," she said, taking the plate from him. "No one has ever served me breakfast."

"Well, I'm happy I was your first."

"You do manage to make yourself useful," she added. Annie dug into the French toast, the scent of vanilla making her hungrier than she'd thought she was. "If you wash floors and windows, I might just have to ask you to stay."

He stopped eating for a moment and met her gaze. "I could stay if you wanted me to."

Annie felt her face flame with embarrassment.

She was just teasing. "I—I— You have better things to do with your time, I'm sure."

"Actually, I don't," he said with a shrug. "I'm currently between jobs. I quit my last job to come up here and handle Buddy's estate. I thought I might like living on the island, but it wasn't for me."

"Can you go back to your old job?" she asked.

Rourke shook his head. "No chance of that. I kind of burned my bridges there."

"Where did you work?"

"At the company my father founded."

"Don't you want to work with your father anymore?"

"He died," Rourke said. "About eight years ago. I continued on there after he was gone because I didn't want all his hard work to go to waste. But his partners didn't share my vision for the company. When Buddy died, I decided I needed a new direction in my life, so I quit."

"And you came here. But island life doesn't suit you, does it."

He drew a deep breath. Now he seemed to be a bit embarrassed. "It's a pretty lonely existence."

"Yes, I guess it is." Annie nodded. "No sex. I know. It is a little tricky. You just have to seize the opportunity when it presents itself. *Carpe sexum.*"

"You could always take Sam up on his offer," Rourke said, grinning.

"I could. But he and I have a past. And I don't trust him." Annie took another bite of her breakfast. "And he lives here. If things went bad, it would be…uncomfortable."

"We have a past, too," Rourke said.

Annie swirled a piece of her French toast in a pool of maple syrup, her mind drifting back to that day. "Yes, we do," she murmured.

"I'm not talking about the bullies," he said. "I'm talking about last night. We have a past now."

Drawing a deep breath, she met his gaze. "I suppose now we're going to have the talk about what it all means."

To her surprise, Rourke shook his head. "I know what it means to me. That's enough for now."

She frowned. His cryptic statement begged for further explanation, but Annie had never been one to delve too deeply into emotional matters. "Good," she murmured, turning back to her breakfast.

In truth, her emotional connection to him frightened her. She'd been so careful to keep her distance—from men, from the residents on the island, from anyone who might try to carve out a place in her life. It was safer to be alone, with only her own happiness to worry about.

They finished eating in an uncomfortable silence, Annie wondering what was going on inside Rourke's head. It was clear he'd enjoyed their night together. And that he wanted more of the same. But was he beginning to doubt the wisdom of their decision? If he wasn't, Annie certainly had her own set of fears and insecurities.

What if she couldn't just let him walk out of her life? What if tomorrow was like today and all she could think about were reasons to make him stay? When she was with him she felt alive, as if her heart had suddenly begun to beat again and she was aware of every breath she drew. Was this what love felt like?

After so much loss in her life, Annie had hardened herself against such a dangerous emotion. First her mother, then her father, had abandoned her, leaving her to fend for herself, watched over by a grandmother who refused to even acknowledge the existence of her parents.

This was how love began. Even she knew that. With desire and passion, with emotions raging out of control. If she wasn't careful, she'd be swallowed up, just like her mother and father, so consumed with it that she'd rather die than live without it.

Her fingers trembled as she reached for her coffee mug. Maybe it would be best to send him on his way. As soon as the storm calmed, she'd find some excuse to get him out of the house and back on the road.

"What are you going to do when you get back

home?" she asked. "I mean, if you don't have a job?"

"I don't know," Rourke replied. "I suppose I'll have to look for a new job."

"What do you do? I mean, for a living?"

"I'm a civil engineer. My father was president of a consulting firm. We help to retrofit buildings to be safer during natural disasters like earthquakes and hurricanes. My dad and I were really close. And he was so proud that I wanted to be a part of the business he started."

"What about your mom?"

Rourke shrugged. "She took the money from my father's life insurance and found herself a new husband. She was quite a bit younger than he was. Actually, she was his secretary before she was his wife." He reached out and took her plate, then wandered back to the kitchen. "We see each other at Christmas and we usually go out to dinner on my birthday, but she's really more interested in her new husband than me. Trying to keep him happy, I guess."

"I'm sorry to hear about your father. And I was sad when I heard Buddy had died. He was a nice man. He was always kind to me. Whenever he saw me on my bike, he'd pull over and insist on giving me a ride. He'd toss my bike in the back of that old red pickup and off we'd go. I used to ride over to his house during the summer and I'd help him weed his garden. He grew the best tomatoes. We'd sit on his porch and eat them, warm from the sun."

Rourke sat down on the hearth, stretching his legs out in front of him. "I didn't know that."

Annie nodded. "We were both kind of lonely, I guess."

"I should have come to see him more often," he said, shaking his head. "I just figured he'd live forever, he was such a tough old guy."

She reached out and pressed her hand to his cheek. "I saw you at the funeral," Annie murmured.

"You were there?"

"Yeah. I watched from the woods."

"Why?"

She shrugged. There were always explanations and justifications for her odd behavior. But with Rourke, she felt as if, with every question, he was peeling away a layer of protection, searching for the soft center inside of her. "It's complicated," she said.

"Tell me."

"Well, I wanted to grieve privately," she began. "I don't like showing my emotions in front of people, especially the people on this island. And most of the folks in town would be watching me for a reaction, wondering if I was suddenly going to start screaming and pulling my hair out."

"They don't think that," Rourke said.

"Don't kid yourself," Annie countered. "They think I'm like my mother, that I take after her side of the family. They remember how she was—irrational, emotional."

"You know what? I think you like it that way. I think you like keeping them at a distance, letting them think you're just a little bit crazy. That way you don't have the responsibility of friendship or the chance at love."

"I have friends," she said.

"But only friends who maintain their distance. I'd call them acquaintances."

Annie pulled her knees up to her chest, wrapping her arms around her legs. "Maybe that's true. That's just the way I am. I don't need friends."

In truth, Annie had wondered if they might be right. Would she turn out like her mother? Would she suddenly snap and retreat into a world of her own, a world filled with fears and paranoia one day and giddy euphoria the next? A world where she couldn't distinguish reality from fantasy?

"Everyone needs friends," Rourke said. "You do. I think you'd like to have people smile at you when you walk into the hardware store, or wave at you from across the street."

Annie stood up, wrapping the quilt more tightly around her naked body. "Can we stop with the psychoanalysis, Dr. Freud?" She snatched her coffee mug from the hearth and walked over to the sink.

"Just because you made me breakfast doesn't mean you can tell me how to live my life."

Rourke followed her to the kitchen, slipping his arms around her waist and slowly turning her to face him. He took the edges of the quilt between his fingers and slowly parted the faded patchwork, revealing her body beneath.

Annie shivered as the quilt dropped onto the plank floor. Slowly, he drew his hands over her naked body, smoothing the gentle curve of her shoulders and the length of her arms, then moving up from her waist to her breasts. Her breath caught when he teased at her nipples with his thumbs, the cold and his caress drawing them to a hard peak.

"Do you want me to leave?" he whispered, his head dipping lower to steal a quick kiss. "I'll leave, just say the word."

His hand slipped from her breast and, palm flat, skimmed down her stomach to the spot between her legs. He teased her there, with a gentle flick of his fingers, and Annie closed her eyes at the wave of sensation that raced through her. With every other man, she'd been able to maintain her self-control. Why was Rourke Quinn different? Why did her body seem to crave his touch?

"Say the word," he repeated, his fingers gently rubbing between the soft folds of her sex.

"No," she gasped, leaning against him as a wave of pleasure washed over her. "Don't leave."

THE STORM CONTINUED through the day, the rain battering the cottage and the wind whistling through the shutters. They stayed in bed, taking the time to test the boundaries of their desire for each other.

Rourke was surprised at how uninhibited Annie was when it came to sex. Though she refused to surrender to emotion, she didn't have any problem surrendering to passion. Most women couldn't tell the two apart, but Annie had a firm grasp on that. Unfortunately, he was finding the task a bit more difficult than usual.

It was hard not to feel something for her. She had an empty spot deep inside her heart and he just wanted to fill it with good feelings, with happiness and contentment, with optimism. She deserved at least that much after such a difficult childhood. But who was he to swoop in and try to change her life with just a few nights in bed?

Her naked body was curled up against his, her fingers splayed on his chest. He turned his face into her silky hair and drew a deep breath. She smelled of lavender soap and wood smoke.

Rourke closed his eyes. There was no reason he couldn't stay a little longer. He had a place to live until he decided what to do with his uncle's cottage and he wasn't anxious to get back to New York. He'd sublet his apartment until after the holidays and had planned to camp out on a friend's sofa until he'd decided what to do next. Why not do his deciding here?

Annie stirred beside him and her hand slipped beneath the quilt, resting on his belly. "Are you awake?" she whispered.

"Mmm-hmm."

"I thought so. I could hear the wheels turning in your head." She pushed up on her elbow and looked down at him, her expression sleepy and satisfied. "You think too much."

Rourke reached out and tucked her tumbled hair behind her ear. "Yeah, well, I guess that's the way I'm wired. Am I supposed to not care about you?"

"Yes," she said. "This was supposed to be just sex."

"Well, maybe I like you. Maybe I think you're funny and beautiful and strange and inscrutable and—"

"I'm inscrutable?"

"You are…a bit difficult to figure out. But I enjoy the challenge. And I enjoy being with you. So, no, it isn't just about the sex. At least not for me. And you know what? I don't care what you think about that."

"Gee, well, you certainly did tell me," Annie said, her eyebrow arched, her words laced with sarcasm.

He heard the defensive young girl in her voice and knew he'd pushed her too far. But he didn't care. "And I plan to keep telling you," Rourke added, tossing the covers aside and crawling out of bed. He grabbed his jeans from the floor and tugged them on. "We need more wood."

"No, we don't," she said.

"All right, I need to get more wood." He turned to face her. "For a woman I barely know, you sure know how to push my buttons. You know, I really wish you had a television. Right now, I could use a good football game."

Kit stood at the door, his tail wagging, his gaze expectant. Rourke grabbed his jacket and slipped his bare feet into his boots, then walked outside, slamming the door behind him. Rourke stood on the porch, the hard rain stinging his skin. The ice from the night before had already melted, but there was still a chill in the air.

He moved to grab some wood, then froze, his gaze fixed on a spot at the bottom of the porch steps. At first he thought it was some sort of debris, blown in by the storm. But then it blinked at him and he found himself staring into dark, liquid eyes. "Jaysus," he muttered to the seal. "Where did you come from?"

Kit bounded out into the rain, not even bothering to stop and sniff at the seal. Rourke slowly backed up toward the door. The seal looked perfectly healthy. In truth, it looked as if it was just hanging around, waiting for someone to come outside.

He reached for the door and slipped back in the house. Annie had pulled on a sweater and jeans and was standing next to the hearth, poking at the embers.

"We have a visitor," Rourke said.

"Is Sam back?"

"No. There's a seal outside. Just sitting there at the bottom of the steps."

A slow smile broke across her face. "She's back!" Annie grabbed her jacket and tugged on her boots, then rushed past him to the door. Rourke followed her outside and found her, her hand outstretched to the animal.

"Be careful," Rourke warned.

"Don't worry," Annie said. "We're old friends. I've been waiting for her."

The herring. That's what she'd come to the hardware store to buy. He glanced around and saw a bucket sitting on the corner of the porch. He walked over and lifted the lid. The scent of fish wafted into the chilly air. He grabbed the handle and carried it down the steps, setting it beside her.

Annie plucked a fish from the bucket and held it up. The seal arched its neck and grabbed the herring from her hand, swallowing it in one gulp. As Rourke watched her, he barely even noticed the cold and the rain and the wind. For the first time since he had arrived on her doorstep, she seemed completely happy.

Rourke sat down beside her and pulled her hood up over her damp hair. Her hands were red with cold, yet she continued to hold herring out to the seal. She handed him a fish and he dropped it into the creature's mouth. After about ten minutes and a half bucket of herring, the seal suddenly turned and flopped its way back toward the water.

Annie stood and watched it until it disappeared from view. Droplets of water trickled down her cheeks and Rourke knew that they were tears, not rain. He grabbed her cold hands and held them between his. "Will she be back?"

Annie nodded. "Tomorrow…I hope." She turned and walked to the door, leaving it open behind her.

"Should we leave Kit out?" he called.

"Let him run," she said. "He'll scratch on the door when he wants to come in."

The cabin seemed warm and cozy compared to the chill of the storm. "How do you know that seal?"

"Three years ago, I found her lying between the rocks. She was starving and maybe sick. And I nursed her back to health. Now every year, right about this time, she shows up to say hello. Just like clockwork. Always the first week in October. I buy herring and feed her. And then she disappears for another year. I wasn't sure she'd come again. She should be old enough to have pups now. Once she does, I think she'll stop coming." She paused. "I know I shouldn't have named her, but I call her Lady Gray."

"Where does she go when she leaves?"

"There's a gray seal colony over on Hay Island." Annie shrugged out of her jacket and hung it up. "That's where the seal hunt takes place." She shook her head. "I'm just glad when she shows up. Seals can live to be forty years old if a predator doesn't get them first. Forty years."

Rourke smiled. God, could she be any sweeter? Saving starving seals. He stepped toward her and pulled her into his arms, drawing her into a long, deep kiss. He cupped her face in his hands, then pulled back. "I smell like fish," he said.

Annie giggled, then held her hand in front of his nose. "Me, too."

A scratch sounded at the door and Rourke opened it. Kit bounded in, then jumped up, placing his paws on Rourke's chest and licking his face.

"Down, Kit," Annie commanded. "Get down."

"Great," Rourke muttered. "Now I smell like dead fish and dog drool. If you'd like to throw up on me, we'd have a hat trick." He let his jacket drop to the floor. "I could use a shower."

"Why don't you put on the pot for tea and I'll go out and turn the water heater on in the lighthouse. In another hour, you can have your shower."

"You, too," Rourke said. "You don't smell like a rose."

"The water heater is pretty small. Only enough for one shower."

"Then we'll just have to shower together," he said, sending her his most charming grin.

"All right," she said. "I'll be right back."

"And I'll be waiting," Rourke said.

He stepped out onto the porch and watched her cross the windswept rise to the lighthouse. The wind had calmed a bit and didn't threaten to blow her off her feet. When she reached the door of the lighthouse, he grabbed a few more logs from the pile on the porch, then stepped back into the warmth of the cabin.

The fire in the stove was almost out, but with a bit of tending, he managed to get it going again. He washed his hands in water from the pitcher sitting next to the sink, but no amount of soap would completely rid him of the fishy smell.

He stood at the sink and smiled to himself. This wasn't such a bad life, he mused. A guy could get used to the quiet. And did he really need all his electronic toys? His iPod and laptop were in the car, but he certainly didn't need them. Without the constant distraction, he had time to think. And his mind was surprisingly clear and focused.

He wasn't foolish enough to believe that Annie wasn't a part of this odd contentment he'd found.

They'd known each other for a day and yet it seemed as if they'd been together for years. He knew her, completely and intimately. Not the silly, trivial facts, like her favorite color or her preferred brand of shampoo. He knew her heart: deep inside of her was a woman who wanted to be loved.

He'd told her she was inscrutable, and it might take longer than a day to figure out how her mind worked. In truth, that's what he found so fascinating about her. She was one of a kind. And he'd always thought, when he found the right woman, that's exactly what he wanted.

THE HOT WATER washed over her and Annie felt his fingers in her hair, gently massaging the shampoo into her scalp. Though she'd tried to tell him to hurry, Rourke wasn't hearing any of it. This wasn't a big-city hotel with an endless supply of hot water. They had about ten minutes and that was it.

Annie leaned back against him, her backside brushing up against his growing erection. For the first time in a long time, she wished they were in the city, in some luxurious hotel with heat and running water and expensive bed linens. Oh, and room service. Food and drink delivered right to the door.

She turned and began to rinse her hair. "You'd better hurry," she said. "We've got about three minutes left."

He reached out and cupped her breast in his palm. "God, you are beautiful," he murmured.

She opened her eyes and looked up at him. "You can admire me later." Bending over, she grabbed the bottle of shampoo and squeezed a bit into her hand. Then she reached up and rubbed it into his hair. Rourke grabbed her waist and pulled her against him, his shaft pressing into her belly.

She reached down to stroke him with her soapy hand. He moaned softly, arching into her touch. But as he came closer and closer to his release, the water from the shower began to cool. Finally, Annie was forced to step out from under the spray, leaving him on the edge.

"Quick, rinse your hair," she said.

Cursing softly, Rourke leaned into the cold water and did as he was told. Annie held out a towel for him and, shuddering, he quickly dried his face. Annie turned, her hair still dripping. She slipped her feet into her wellies.

"Where are you going?" Rourke asked.

"Back to the cottage," she said.

"Like that?"

"Why put clothes on when you're just going to take them off again?" She let her eyes drift down to his stiff shaft. She smiled. "Let's see if you can handle it."

"I'm not going out there naked," he said.

Annie shrugged. "Then get dressed." She went

outside and the cold hit her skin like a million pin-pricks. The rain had stopped and all that was left of the storm was a damp wind blowing off the water. She drew a deep breath and then ran across the rise to the house. Kit saw her and raced up to run beside her, jumping up in his excitement. When she reached the house, she turned back and saw Rourke following her, slipping on the muddy grass, dressed only in his boots.

She laughed as he took the porch steps two at a time and they both tumbled into the house. Kit scampered in behind them, getting tangled in their feet for a moment before Annie ordered him over to his spot in front of the fire.

His hands seemed to be everywhere, searching for favorite spots on her body, sending wild sensations coursing to her core. No matter what he did, it didn't seem to be enough to satisfy her. Now that they'd shared the ultimate intimacy, that's what she wanted—Rourke…moving inside her.

But to her dismay, he didn't seem to be in any hurry to get to that part of the seduction. Instead, he backed her up against the edge of the table, then drew her leg up along his hip until he was pressing temptingly close to the moist spot between her legs.

She moved against him, but he shifted, as if he knew that slipping inside her would be the end instead of the beginning. Taking some satisfaction in the fact that she was able to bring him to the edge so quickly and to tease him further, she reached down and wrapped her fingers around him.

"You're a very dangerous lady," he whispered. "I can't seem to control myself when I touch you. Or when you touch me."

"I think that's a good thing," Annie said.

"Not if we want to make this last all night long," he said.

Annie gasped. "All night?"

"Why not? Do you have any plans for tomorrow?"

"No."

He reached around her, then picked Annie up and set her on the edge of the old wooden table. "Good. Because I'm just getting started."

Rourke tugged her boots off and threw them at the door, then kicked out of his own. Though the cottage was chilly, it didn't matter. In truth, it seemed to heighten every sensation—the feel of his soft lips on her nipple, the warmth of his tongue, the scrape of his beard against her belly. It was almost too much to bear.

She felt so exposed, lying on her kitchen table, naked and open to his touch. But for the first time in her memory, she wasn't afraid to be vulnerable. Though she hadn't known Rourke long, she knew she could trust him. He seemed to genuinely care for her happiness—and for her sexual satisfaction.

He focused his attention on the spot between her legs and she felt wave after wave of pleasure wash over her. Her body pulsed with need and just when she thought he was ready to take her over the edge, he slowed his pace.

Frustrated, Annie decided to do the same to him. She pushed up on her elbows, then placed her bare foot on his shoulder, gently nudging him away. "Stop," she murmured.

He looked up at her. "I'm just getting started."

Annie slid to the edge of the table, then hopped down. "No, *I'm* just getting started." She grabbed his arms and turned him around, pushing him up against the table.

She began with a touch, gentle at first, her fingers stroking his shaft slowly as she trailed kisses over his chest. Lingering over his nipple, Annie was rewarded with a gasp, then a groan, before he wove his fingers through the hair at her nape.

As she moved lower, he tried to stop her, pulling her back to kiss her once again. But Annie didn't want to play by his rules all the time. She wanted a bit of control.

When her lips closed over him, she felt his body jerk, but she wasn't deterred. She slowly seduced him with her tongue and her lips, taking him into her mouth in a deliberate rhythm. At some point, he gave up any resistance and allowed himself to submit. Annie felt as if she was learning what pleased him with every minute that passed. It felt so good to know a man so intimately. It made her feel like a powerful, attractive woman…not like the Annie that everyone thought they knew.

She wasn't that shy, scared girl anymore. If she wanted this man, she could have him—any way she wanted him. And right now, Annie wanted him in her bed, his naked body stretched out on top of hers.

Slowly straightening, she kissed her way back to his lips, then wrapped her arms around his neck, her tongue teasing at his. Rourke chuckled softly as she rubbed up against him, continuing to torment him. But then he grabbed her hips and picked her up, and she locked her legs around his body.

"I guess that run through the cold night was exactly what I needed."

"Did it wake you up?" she asked.

"When I'm with you, the last thing I'm thinking about is sleep."

"Then take me to bed," Annie said. She slipped out of his embrace and moved toward the warmth and comfort that awaited them beneath the faded old quilts.

She'd grown to love the feel of his naked body against hers, their limbs tangled together so that she couldn't tell where he left off and she began. He pulled the quilts up over them both, then rolled her beneath him, bracing his weight on his outstretched arms.

"This is getting to be a habit," he murmured, his dark gaze fixed on hers. "A habit I don't want to break."

They'd been living in the moment, with Annie knowing that it could end at any time. But she'd reached a point where she didn't want to think about the end, about standing on her porch and waving goodbye as he drove off into the distance. She wanted to believe that they'd have many more nights just like this one.

He rolled to his side and retrieved the box of condoms from the bedside table, allowing Annie to slip the latex sheath over his hard shaft. She held her breath as he slowly entered her, the anticipation all she had imagined.

From the very first moment of their joining, she knew that this would be different. With every thrust, she felt herself dancing with the fringes of her control. He began slowly, but then his strokes grew deeper and faster.

Annie felt her body betray her, felt her fingertips and toes begin to tingle. When the spasms shook her body, they took her by surprise and she couldn't stop herself. But as if he was waiting for a sign, Rourke pulled her hips against his and thrust once more before following her over the edge.

It seemed to go on forever and when Annie

could finally think rationally again, she found herself oddly frightened. How would she ever do without this? How could she sleep in this bed alone and not want him here with her, driving her to the edges of desire, possessing her body and her soul?

She had dealt with so much loss in her life, yet all of it had been out of her control. But this was one thing she could control. If she wanted him to stay, she could ask him to stay. Every night could be like this night.

4

THE STORM WAS winding down outside. The wind was merely a breeze now and the rain had stopped hours ago. After another round of incredible sex, they fixed dinner together.

Rourke had opened the shutters, but once the sun went down, the inside of the cottage was cast in the soft light from the oil lamps. Annie was curled up in her chair next to the fire, reading a book of Whitman's poetry out loud as he finished the dinner dishes.

It was nearly midnight, but neither one of them was thinking about sleep. In truth, Rourke didn't want to sleep. If this was the last night they spent together, he wanted to enjoy every minute of it.

He glanced over his shoulder at Annie, snuggled up beneath a crocheted throw, her hands kept warm by fingerless gloves. There were so many things he wanted to say to her, yet he was afraid he'd scare her off. If he'd learned anything over the past two days, he knew when to speak and when to hold his tongue.

He'd have to wait until she asked him to stay another night. She'd asked him not to leave but that had been heat of the moment. He worried that if he made the offer to stay now, she'd balk. Her brow would furrow and she'd give him a suspicious look, then explain once again that he would be leaving the island once he finally left her bed.

"The weather's looking better," he said, folding the dish towel and setting it next to the sink.

"These storms usually blow themselves out after a couple days."

"I noticed that some of the shingles had come off your roof. I'm thinking I'll run into town tomorrow and get some materials so I can patch your roof. You wouldn't want it to leak."

She slowly closed her book. "I thought you'd be leaving in the morning."

"And I'm thinking I might stick around a little longer," Rourke said. He held his breath, waiting for her response. But to his surprise, she merely shrugged.

"Suit yourself."

"I kind of wanted to see if your seal comes back tomorrow."

"She will," Annie said, opening the book again.

Rourke rubbed his hands together, then walked over to the door, peering out the window into the darkness. They'd been cooped up in the cabin for forty-eight hours. He was beginning to get a little restless.

"So what do you do to entertain yourself?" he asked. "I mean, if I wasn't here to entertain you, what would you be doing right now?"

"I read." She held up her book. "Sometimes I write poetry or songs. I sketch. And paint. I sew. I have a loom in the parlor and during the summer, I weave. I garden and take walks in the summer. There's plenty to do."

He shook his head. "And you don't ever get bored?" Rourke crossed the room and sat down across from her in the wooden rocker. Bending forward, he braced his elbows on his knees. "The one thing I'd miss is my music."

"Don't you have one of those iPod things?" she asked.

"Yeah, but that doesn't compare to the sound system I had in my apartment."

With a sigh, she dropped her book on the hearth and stood up. "Grab that lantern. If you want music, I'll get you music."

She opened the door and they stepped into the front half of the first floor. Rourke saw canvases propped up against the walls and he walked over to examine a painting of the lighthouse. He didn't know much about art, but he knew the painting was good.

"You did this?"

Annie nodded. "It's no big deal. Sometimes I trade one of my paintings for firewood. Sam Decker's mother sells them in her shop in town. I heard there's one hanging in the café now. No one knows I painted it, though, so don't say anything around town, okay?"

"Why wouldn't you want people to know?"

"I'm not a painter. I don't want everyone thinking that I am and asking me to paint something for them."

"It's a good way to make money," he said.

"I don't need more money," Annie replied.

Rourke bit back a curse. Why was she so afraid to want things in her life? Though she acted as if she was perfectly happy, he could imagine how difficult it was to eke out a living without any visible means of income. Why not sell a few more paintings and get some electricity in her place, or running water?

"I'd buy one of your paintings," he said.

She drew a sheet off a tall, square-shaped cabinet. "Here it is. Help me move it."

The cabinet was on wheels and they rolled it to the door and into the warmth of the kitchen. Annie opened the top to reveal an old Victrola. Then she pulled the cabinet door open and grabbed a record. "Remember these?" she asked.

"Records? Or 78s?"

"Records," she said. She put the record on the turntable then took a crank handle out of the cabinet and stuck it into a hole in the side of the Victrola. "You wanted music. You have to wind it up."

Rourke turned the crank and then flipped the lever and the record began to spin. He carefully dropped the needle on the edge of the vinyl and a few seconds later, the sound of an aria filled the tiny room.

"And we have music," she said, plopping down into her chair near the fire.

Rourke had never heard anything quite so beautiful as that pure, perfect voice coming out of the old speaker. He pulled more of the recordings from the cabinet and sorted through them. When he found a few big-band recordings he turned off the opera singer and replaced her with Artie Shaw.

"I love this one," Annie said, smiling. "'Begin The Beguine.' I always wondered just what a beguine was."

"Don't look at me. I don't have a clue." Rourke swayed over to her and pulled her to her feet. "It does kind of make you want to dance, doesn't it?"

They made a few passes around the room before he pulled her down into the chair, settling her on his lap. "I want to take you out," he said.

"Outside?"

"No. Out. On a date. Tomorrow night. We'll find a nice restaurant and have a meal that neither one of us has to cook. There's a really good pizzeria in Port Hawkesbury. Not fancy, but great pizza."

Annie shook her head. "I don't know."

"No one knows you there. We'll just be two regular people having a pizza and a few beers. It will be fun."

He could see her searching for an excuse not to go. But in the end, she shrugged. "All right. I like pizza. It won't be as good as mine, but I'll try to keep an open mind."

Rourke chuckled. "Good idea." He pulled her close and kissed her. Annie wrapped her arms around his neck and snuggled closer. For a long time, they did nothing but kiss. And though it was tempting to pick her up and take her to bed, he decided that he'd managed to take a very big step forward in getting her to agree to dinner out. He'd let her make the next move.

"Do you think we could go out for ice cream, too?" she asked.

"Sure."

"I don't get ice cream a lot. If I carry it home on my bike, it usually melts. In the summer, I ride into town and buy a pint at the supermarket and sit in the park and eat it all before I ride home."

Rourke chuckled. "You really are the oddest girl I've ever met."

"But odd in a good way, right?" She laced her fingers through his and drew his hand closer, letting it come to rest against her heart.

"Are you warm enough?" he asked, his lips brushing against hers. "I could put another log on the fire."

"I'm quite snug," she said, wriggling into his body.

He'd bought himself another night and without any discussion of when he planned to leave the island. She seemed almost resigned to the fact that he'd decided to stay.

Rourke smoothed his hand down the length of her leg and grabbed her foot, encased in a heavy wool sock. He gently massaged it, rubbing his thumbs into the arch. Annie sighed and smiled. "That's nice.

She studied him silently as he focused on her feet and he knew something was on her mind. Finally she spoke. "I wanted to ask… Why did you come here before the storm?"

"I told you, I was worried about the weather. I wanted to make sure you were safe."

"Was that all?"

Rourke wondered what she was getting at. "I didn't expect this," he said. "I just figured I'd help you board up a few windows and move some things indoors." He paused. "And maybe I was curious."

"About what?"

"You. I remembered you from years ago. And when I saw you again, I wanted to make sure you were…happy."

"And am I?"

"Yes," Rourke said. "I'm happy to see that you are happy. You're fine."

She leaned close and kissed him, a kiss that began softly and sweetly. But Rourke wanted more. He slipped his fingers through the hair at her nape and began a gentle assault on her mouth, tempting her to surrender. Once he possessed her lips, then he'd move on to her body—her breasts, her belly, the long, sweet length of her legs.

For a woman who'd been through so much in her life, she seemed remarkably resilient. It was that inner strength that he found so attractive. She knew exactly who she was and what she wanted from life. And though she didn't possess many of the creature comforts, she was content.

What did that feel like? Rourke wondered. Since his father's death, he hadn't felt satisfied with his own life. No one knew whether they would be alive tomorrow, and he hadn't started living yet. He'd spent most of his adult life searching for something that would make him happy. Maybe he'd found it here, in this windswept cottage on this isolated spit of land…with this beautiful woman.

ANNIE OPENED HER eyes to a pounding that just didn't want to go away. She rubbed her temple, wondering if it was just a leftover from some strange dream. But as she sat up in bed, she realized that the sound was coming from overhead.

Grabbing the quilt from the bed, she wrapped it around herself and crawled out of bed. Kit was gone and so was Rourke. She glanced at the clock hanging over the sink and saw that she'd slept away most of the morning.

He'd left the pot of coffee warming on the stove and she poured herself a mug before stepping outside onto the porch. A ladder was propped up against the edge of the porch roof and a few seconds later, she saw his legs, then the rest of his body as he descended the ladder.

"Hey," he said, his face breaking into a wide smile. "You're up. I was wondering if you were going to sleep all day."

Annie ran her hand through her tangled hair. Even completely dressed, his hair windblown and his face shadowed by the stubble of a two-day beard, he was drop-dead sexy. "What are you doing?"

"I'm doing the prep work to fix your roof," he said.

"You don't have to do that," she murmured.

He sauntered over and slipped his hands around her waist. His lips brushed against hers, then lingered for a deeper kiss. "I thought maybe we could work out a trade," he murmured.

"What do you want to trade?" Annie asked, giggling as his mouth trailed down to her throat. A shiver skittered down her spine and she felt that familiar thrill that his touch elicited.

"I don't know. I'll have to think about it. Maybe another night like last night?"

"You don't have to trade for that. I like to do that free," she said.

He drew back and looked down at her. "Yeah?"

"Yeah," she said. "Of course, that does have to do with your considerable skill in the sack."

"I am good, aren't I?"

"Yes, you are very good."

Rourke kissed her again. "You bring out the best in me." He nuzzled her neck, then stepped away. "I need to finish the shingling," he explained. "And then I'm going to buy some insulation and install it in the attic. The house would be much warmer if it were insulated better."

"No, that's too much," she said. "I can't afford that."

"Don't worry about it. You can give me a painting." He strolled down the front steps, grinning to himself.

Annie frowned. She'd always paid her own way and taken great pride in the fact that she owed no one. This didn't feel right. He'd said otherwise, but did he really expect that she'd repay him in the bedroom? Was that what this was about?

"No!" she called as he started to climb the ladder.

Rourke paused. "What?"

"No," Annie repeated. "To the insulation. No insulation. I can't afford it."

"You can't not afford it. It will save money on the firewood you use. And while I'm at it, I should put all new windows in the cottage. They're so leaky that there's no way to keep that room warm."

"It's fine the way it is," Annie insisted. "Please, just fix the roof and that's all." She turned and walked back into the cottage, closing the door behind her.

But Rourke wasn't about to let the subject rest. A few seconds later he walked inside, his expression tense, his gaze dark. "Why don't we just have this out right now, okay?"

"I told you what I wanted. There's nothing to talk about."

"Is it that you don't think you deserve for people to do nice things for you? Or are you just so controlling that you can't accept any help at all? Because, personally, I'd like to know so I don't keep running into these brick walls when I'm with you."

"I don't need anyone to take care of me, or fix my roof, or buy insulation for my attic. I'm fine all on my own."

Rourke cursed beneath his breath. "Yes, I'm aware of that. You've proved that beyond a shadow of a doubt. But that doesn't mean you can't graciously accept help when it's offered."

"I don't need charity."

"This isn't charity," he retorted.

Annie felt her emotions surge and she fought against the tears that threatened. Didn't he understand how difficult this was for her? She'd been alone for so long, suspicious of everyone around her. It wasn't easy to trust anyone, not even the man she'd invited into her bed.

"I don't have to explain myself," she muttered.

"No, you don't. But maybe you might like to. Annie, we can't move forward if you don't tell me what you're really feeling. This doesn't have anything to do with the damn insulation. Tell me why this bothers you."

She crossed the room to her favorite chair and sat down, pulling the blanket more tightly around her body, as if it might offer a shield against his affection. Why not tell him? He'd be gone soon enough and it wouldn't make a difference once he was.

"It's—it's really difficult for me to trust people."

"I know that," he said.

"And because I couldn't trust people when I was younger, because I shut everyone out, I never really learned to read the signs."

"What signs?"

"When someone is lying to me or when his or her motives might not be good." Annie drew a ragged breath. Now that she'd started, she didn't want to stop. Why not tell him everything? "When I was in high school, a boy invited me to the winter formal. He was kind of a quiet boy, not very popular at school. But he seemed nice and I really wanted to wear a long dress and have someone buy me a wrist corsage. I wanted a boy to kiss me and to treat me like I wasn't the strange girl in school."

He stared at her for a long time, his anger fading to be replaced by regret. "I'm not going to want to hear this, am I?"

"My grandmother didn't have money to buy me a new dress, but we found a beautiful party dress that my mother had once worn. It had a velveteen bodice and a skirt made of tulle and it was the prettiest shade of green."

"It went with your eyes," he murmured.

Annie nodded, smiling. "It did. And I felt beautiful for the first time in my life. And then one of the girls at school told me that the bullies had paid this boy to ask me and that he was just not going to show up the night of the dance. He was going to leave me waiting."

This time Rourke cursed out loud. "Who was this kid? Does he still live on the island? Because I'm thinking I might have to beat the shit out of him."

"That's not the point," she said.

"It damn well is. Was it Decker who set this all up? Was he the ringleader?"

"The point is that I should have been able to read the signs. I should have suspected that something was up. But I didn't have the…intuition. I wasn't a very perceptive girl. And I really wanted to believe that my prince had come."

"So now you just mistrust everyone you meet?"

She shrugged, forcing a smile. "Yeah, pretty much."

"And you think that my wanting to insulate your attic is some kind of trick?"

When he said it that way, Annie realized how ridiculous it sounded. "No, of course not. But I don't always think things out before I react. When something confuses me, I just throw the walls up and wait for the bombs to start dropping."

"And do they?"

Annie thought about his question for a long moment, then shook her head. "Not since that day."

"You can trust me," Rourke said. He crossed the room and sat down on the hearth, then reached out and took her hands. Pressing her fingers to his lips, he stared into her eyes. "I would never, ever do anything to hurt you, Annie. If you believe one thing in this life, believe in that."

"You might not even know you're doing it." Her voice caught in her throat, betraying the emotion behind her words.

"And that's why you need to talk to me and tell me how you feel. As much as I'd like to, I can't read your thoughts."

Maybe it was time, Annie thought to herself. Sooner or later, she'd have to take a risk in life. And she felt safe with Rourke. She believed that he did care about her. And even if she got hurt in the end, at least she would have tried. She couldn't live inside a protective shell for the next fifty years. If she did, she'd always be alone.

"All right," she said. "You can insulate my attic."

He slipped his hand around the back of her neck, tangling his fingers in her hair, then pulled her into a kiss. Annie felt her resistance crumble and she pulled him back onto the bed with her.

"I should finish the roof," he murmured, smoothing the hair out of her eyes.

"That can wait," she said. She ran her fingertips over his lower lip, then kissed him.

The kiss dissolved into a frantic seduction and it wasn't long before she'd rid him of his clothes. And when he pulled her legs tight around his hips and sank deep inside of her, Annie knew that she was lost. Even if she wanted to fight this, to resist his charms, she couldn't. He owned her, body and soul, and there was nothing she could do about it.

ROURKE SNIFFED AT his hands. No matter how hard he'd scrubbed them, in the kitchen sink and in the shower in the lighthouse, the smell of fish still lingered.

Lady Gray had returned that afternoon, waiting patiently at the bottom of the porch steps for Annie to appear. The sun had come out for a short time and he and Annie had enjoyed the turn in the weather as they'd fed the seal.

He stood, his hands braced on the porch railing, his gaze fixed on the sea. She had a beautiful piece of property. The views of the small cove and the North Atlantic were stunning and the picturesque old lighthouse only added to the landscape.

If he had any money, he'd build a beautiful house right on the spot. He'd design it himself and he'd make it a green house, using all the most environmentally advanced products. He closed his eyes and tried to picture it. The layout of the rooms was vague and the facade was unfocused, but there was one thing he could see clearly. Annie.

He'd never really thought about what it might feel like to find that one right girl. He'd always known it was a possibility, that he'd see her on the street or stand next to her in line at a coffee shop. They'd fall in love and get married and that would be it.

But the last place he thought he'd find her was here, on Cape Breton, living in a simple cottage with a border collie and the occasional gray seal. Was Annie the one he was supposed to be waiting for?

The cottage door squeaked and he turned to see Annie standing on the threshold, dressed in the deep green party frock she'd described earlier. She looked so beautiful, she took his breath away.

"It still fits," she said.

"Wow."

"Wow good? Or wow, is that a mistake?"

"Wow good," Rourke said.

"I know it's too fancy for pizza, but I really don't care. This might be the only chance I get to wear it."

"Only if every single guy on the island is blind. Once they see you in that dress, they're going to be lining up at your door."

"That's very kind of you to say. You're a very charming, and credible, liar."

He held out his hand to her and when she took it, Rourke tucked it into the crook of his arm. "I'm not lying. Trust me on this."

She gave him a sideways glance. "I think I will."

When they reached his truck, Rourke opened her door for her and helped her inside, tucking in the tulle skirt before shutting the door. When he slipped behind the wheel, he noticed that she had her hands clutched in her lap.

Rourke took her fingers in his and gave her hand a squeeze. "It's just pizza," he said. "You look like I'm driving you to the dentist."

"I'm overdressed."

"Yes, you are. And I love it. I think you look beautiful and I'm the only one who matters."

"You're quite full of yourself, aren't you?"

"I suppose I am. But I'm sure you'll put me in my place if I get out of hand."

Rourke steered the SUV out onto the main road and turned toward Port Hawkesbury. The town sat on the Strait of Canso, a narrow strip of water that separated Cape Breton Island from the rest of Nova Scotia and the Canadian mainland. On his trips to the island as a kid, the strait was always the marker that told him he was almost to his destination.

He tried to keep the conversation light as they made the thirty-minute drive. After a time, Annie seemed to relax and soon she was smiling and laughing. But when they reached the outskirts of Port Hawkesbury, Rourke decided to change their plans. This was far too important an occasion to leave it to some ordinary pizza parlor.

"I don't think I'm in the mood for pizza," he said.

She turned to face him. "Do you want to go

home? I'm fine with that. I could make dinner and—"

"I'm thinking we should go somewhere a little more elegant."

"I shouldn't have worn this dress," she said. "It was silly."

"No, it's perfect. I'm going to take you to Napoleon's. They have steak and seafood and soft music and a pretty decent wine list. And really good bread. They serve it right from the oven with olive oil."

"Are you sure? We could always just grab a pizza and take it home."

Rourke shook his head. "I have a date with the most beautiful girl on the island. I'm going to show her a good time."

"Yay," she said without a trace of enthusiasm.

There wasn't much chance that Annie would turn into an instant social butterfly after one dinner, and Rourke knew that changing her attitude about socializing would have to be done very slowly.

In truth, he knew that he'd probably be leaving the island soon. This thing with Annie would probably run its course and they'd decide it was time to move on. But he wanted to leave her knowing that she wouldn't be spending the rest of her life shut away in her cottage on the shore. She'd have a few friends, she'd feel comfortable in town and people would be happy to see her.

When they reached the restaurant, Rourke found a place to park on the street. He helped Annie out of the truck, then slipped his arm around her waist. She wore a little satin jacket over the dress and it was no protection against the chill in the air.

The interior of Napoleon's was quiet, the weeknight crowd scattered among the tables in the dining room. Their entrance caused some notice and Annie shifted from foot to foot as they waited at the hostess stand.

"Everyone is looking at me," she said, holding tight to his hand.

"You look gorgeous in that dress."

"I look stupid. I don't know what ever possessed me to put it on."

The hostess appeared a few moments later. "Table for two?" she asked, grabbing a pair of menus.

"Yes," Rourke said.

"No," Annie countered.

"No?"

"I'm not really hungry."

"I love your dress," the hostess said. "Is it vintage?"

The compliment took Annie by surprise and Rourke watched as she grasped for a reply. "Yes," Annie said. "It was my mother's."

"Is it designer?" the hostess asked. "It looks like vintage Dior."

"I think it is," Annie said. "My mother loved pretty things. I'm pretty sure she bought it used."

"Well, it's beautiful," the hostess said.

Annie drew a deep breath, then turned to Rourke. "A table would be good," she said.

They were seated at the window, overlooking the harbor. Rourke ordered a bottle of wine and when it arrived, he held up his glass. "To first dates," he said.

Annie laughed nervously. "It does feel like a first date. I'm so nervous I'm going to make a fool of myself." She took a long sip of her wine and it seemed to relax her a bit.

"Tell me something," Rourke said.

"All right," Annie said. "My shoes are pinching and this dress is kind of scratchy. And I should have worn a bra."

"You're not wearing a bra?" he asked.

"No. Does that make a difference?"

Rourke laughed at how quickly they'd gotten off the subject. "That's not what I meant. Why do you hide yourself away in that cottage? You have so much to offer. You're beautiful and funny and smart. But you don't let anyone see that."

"Everyone already has their ideas about me," she said. "People don't change their minds so easily. Look at my parents. The townsfolk made their decisions about them and nothing will change that. My mother was crazy and my father was delusional."

"But you're not your parents," Rourke said.

"My father was from the island. His family was a very important part of the community. *Beloved* is the word most people used. My mother grew up in Montreal. They met and married and he brought her back here to live. But she was never happy here. She was fragile. Always sick. I didn't know until later that she drank, but she did. Their marriage began to fall apart and everyone blamed her. She was…odd. Like me. An outsider."

"I think you like being an outsider. It gives you an excuse not to move forward with your life." The minute the words were out of his mouth, he wanted to take them back. The look on her face was enough to tell him that he'd overstepped.

"I know," she said, her voice barely a whisper.

Rourke gasped. "You know?"

Annie nodded. "It's just easier. Less…pressure. I keep telling myself that it doesn't matter. And sometimes, it really doesn't. But since you've been here, with me, I realize that I need to make some changes."

"If people knew you, they'd love you, Annie. Just like I do."

She took another sip of her wine, then picked up the menu. "What are we going to order?"

Rourke grabbed his own menu, wondering if she'd really heard what he'd just said. He loved her. The words had come out of his mouth, but he hadn't meant them in *that* way. He loved her wit and her kindness, he loved her imagination and her passion. That's what he'd meant. He loved all those wonderful qualities that she possessed.

It was too early to fall in love, he mused. Maybe lust, but not love. Unless, of course, this was a case of love at first sight. No, he wasn't in love.

"I'm going to have a steak," he said.

This was their first date and Rourke had every intention of securing a second date before the evening was out.

5

THEIR DATE HAD been perfect. They'd enjoyed a long leisurely dinner with interesting conversation. Rourke had talked about his life in New York City and he'd asked Annie about her art. They'd laughed and teased and for the first time in a very long time, Annie felt comfortable around strangers.

Rourke had been very protective the entire evening and Annie knew that he was concerned about her bolting. Maybe he thought the way other people in town did—that she was as unstable as her mother had been. Annie knew that's what they said about her. That's why she kept herself away, alone in her little cottage by the ocean. But she was beginning to realize it wasn't because she wanted solitude. She'd just never met a man interesting enough to lure her into the real world.

They ordered dessert and Annie got apple pie with two scoops of ice cream. Rourke settled for a cup of coffee laced with brandy. She dug into the ice cream, then held out a spoonful to him. "It's so good," she murmured, taking a bite for herself and then licking the spoon.

"You know, it wouldn't be that hard to put electricity in your cottage. You could run a line from the pole at the lighthouse and you'd be able to have a fridge and a water heater and even a computer if you wanted."

"What if I don't want?" Annie asked. "I like my simple life." He sighed softly and she could see the frustration in his eyes. "You think I'm crazy, don't you? Like everyone else in town, you think there's something wrong with me because I choose to live the way I do."

"No," Rourke replied. "I'm just trying to make life easier for you."

"No, you're trying to make life easier for you," she said.

"Me? How is that? I don't live in that cold damp cottage all winter long. I don't squint to read a book by the light from a lantern or have to wake up in the middle of the night to put more wood on the fire so I don't freeze to death."

"No, you don't. So why does it bother you so much?"

"When you care about someone, you want the

best for them. You want them to be safe and comfortable. You want life to be easy for them."

Annie laughed softly and took another bite of her ice cream. "I think what you really want is for me to be like everyone else. But I'm not."

"No, you definitely are not like any woman I know."

"Am I that hard to take?" Annie asked. "Is that why you want to change me?"

Rourke glowered. "I don't want to change you. That's not what this is about. I just want the best for you. I want you to be able eat a damn bowl of ice cream whenever you want."

They sat at the table for a long time, the silence dragging on between them. Annie ate her dessert and Rourke sipped his coffee. Things had been going so well between them and then everything seemed to fall apart in the blink of an eye.

She was too stubborn, too set in her ways. She ought to appreciate what he was offering to do instead of taking it as an insult to the life she led. Why did she always have to be so defensive? There were times when she just wanted to let the walls fall. It got so exhausting trying to hold them up—especially against a force as strong as Rourke Quinn.

"I'm sorry," Annie said. "I don't mean to sound ungrateful."

"I do think you like being the odd girl," Rourke

said. "It keeps people away, people who might want get close to you. You want them to think you're a little crazy because it keeps them at a distance. But if you ask me, you're missing out on so much of what's good in life. Annie, you don't deserve to spend the rest of your life alone."

"I think I'd like to go home now," she murmured. It was so much easier to fight her battles on familiar turf. Wearing this silly dress and acting as if she belonged in this fancy restaurant made her feel weak and vulnerable.

Rourke stood up and grabbed her jacket from the back of her chair, then held it as she slipped her arms into the sleeves. Then he tossed a wad of bills on the table before grabbing her hand and heading for the door.

Annie had to hurry to keep up with his pace and once they reached the street, she thought the argument would start up all over again. But instead, Rourke grabbed her waist and spun her around, pressing her back against the brick wall of the restaurant. His mouth came down on hers in a long, desperate kiss. At first, Annie resisted, but then, as the taste of his mouth worked like a drug on her senses, Annie was forced to surrender.

"Don't ever forget that I care for you, Annie. And that I want the best for you. I've never cared about a woman the way I do about you. And that's saying something."

With that, he turned and walked down the street, disappearing around the corner where they'd left his SUV. Annie took a big gulp of the chilly nighttime air. A shiver rocked her body and she crossed her arms over her chest.

"Annie?"

She spun around to find Sam Decker standing on the sidewalk. It was as if he'd appeared out of nowhere. "Sam! What are you doing here?"

"I stopped by your place earlier and you weren't there. I got a little worried."

"How did you know I was here?" Annie asked.

"I thought you might be with Quinn, so I put out an APB on his car."

She swallowed a gasp. "We were just having some dinner," Annie said.

Sam's gaze slowly took in the dress she was wearing and Annie felt her face warm with embarrassment. What was he thinking? Did he think she looked silly? Was he going to tell the whole town of Pearson Bay what he'd seen?

"I—I really should be going," Annie murmured. "Rourke is waiting. He—he just went ahead to warm up the car. Bye, Sam."

With that, she spun on her heel and ran down the sidewalk. When she reached Rourke's SUV, he was leaning against the passenger-side door, his arms crossed over his chest. "I thought you might have decided to take a cab," he said. "Or walk home."

"I—I just ran into Sam Decker," she said as he opened the door for her.

"Decker? What did he want?"

"He stopped by the cottage and found me gone and was worried. So he tracked us down."

Rourke chuckled, but she could see that he found no humor in the situation. "Well, if you didn't believe me that people are capable of caring about you, now you have proof. Maybe he's the one you'd rather have in your bed."

Annie got into the SUV then grabbed the door handle. "Don't be ridiculous. I told you I don't trust him. And I'm perfectly satisfied with you in my bed. Why would I want someone else?"

He stared at her for a long moment, then shook his head. This time his laugh was genuine. The problem was, Annie wasn't sure what she'd said that was so funny.

"Well, I guess that answers my question," he muttered.

"I guess it does," Annie said. She paused. "What question?"

He closed the door and she watched him as he circled around to the driver's side. Was it any wonder she wanted to avoid any emotional entanglements? They'd known each other three days and their relationship was already a mess. Annie wasn't even sure what they were arguing about.

"What question?" she repeated once he'd slipped behind the wheel.

"I was curious about how you really felt about me."

"Well, you're wrong," Annie said. "You can't possibly know how I feel because I'm not sure how I feel."

"I think you know exactly how you feel. You just refuse to admit it. That way, you can pretend that you have everything under control."

Annie crossed her arms over her chest and sank back into the seat. She had no clue what he wanted from her and she also had no clue what she wanted from him. Why was this suddenly so complicated?

THE NEXT MORNING dawned bright and clear. All traces of the nor'easter had dissolved inland and it was a beautiful autumn day on Cape Breton. Rourke yawned as he steered the SUV toward town.

He'd decided not to consider Annie's opinion when it came to insulating her attic and just do it. What was she going to do, forbid him to climb the attic stairs? Lock him out of the cottage? He'd already learned that it was sometimes better not to risk asking her opinion. Especially if he wanted to avoid any kind of drama.

He fought off another yawn. He hadn't slept much the night before. After they'd returned from the restaurant, they took out their frustrations with each other in bed, enjoying a rollicking roll in the sack that left them both exhausted.

Annie had fallen asleep, but Rourke had been plagued with restlessness. So he'd grabbed the flashlight and gone exploring. He really hadn't intended to violate her privacy, but he'd wanted another look at what was in the front parlor.

He'd barely noticed the chill in the air as he went through her art, piece by piece. He'd seen some of the big oil paintings, the beautiful seascapes and landscapes. But then he'd stumbled upon all sorts of smaller works. There were weavings and quilt squares. There were beautiful Celtic crosses pressed into copper and screen printed onto homemade paper. He'd found a whole series of pen-and-ink drawings of local wildlife and watercolors of wildflowers.

When he'd seen it all, he'd been left breathless at the depth and scope of her work. She'd even taken some of her poems and turned them into handmade greeting cards—cards that were more beautiful and touching than any he could find in a store.

All that talent and no one knew about it. Rourke was afraid to bring it up, afraid that she'd be angry at him for snooping. But if she was looking for a source of income, it was sitting in her front parlor. All of her art was salable. She could give it to a gallery or a gift shop on the island and make enough to pay for central heat in the cottage or indoor plumbing or electricity. He just had to convince her to take the chance.

Rourke pulled up in front of the hardware store and hopped out of the truck. When he walked inside, Betty Gillies was behind the counter to welcome him.

"Well, hello again. Are you ever leaving town or have you decided to take up residence in Pearson Bay?"

"Oh, I'll be going soon enough," Rourke replied. "I've got a few more things keeping me busy."

He hadn't mentioned that he was staying at Annie's place, but he was sure that most of the townsfolk already knew. Nothing was truly private on the island. You couldn't sneeze without someone on the other side of town calling it pneumonia.

"A few more things? Or is it Annie Macintosh who's keeping you busy?" Betty chuckled. "What can I get ya? More of those shingles?"

"Nope, this time it's insulation," Rourke said. "Ten rolls ought to do it. The same stuff you sold me for Buddy's place."

"Speaking of Buddy's place, I've had a few inquiries about it. Not to buy, but to rent for next week."

"Why would someone want to rent it for a week?" Rourke asked.

"The Celtic Colors music festival starts next week. Every hotel and motel room on the island is taken. Some folks rent their houses out. My cousins are comin' in from Toronto and rather than sleep on my floor, they were hoping to rent a place."

"Sure, I guess we could do that. I have no idea what to charge, though."

"Marcy O'Neill is renting out her cottage. Why don't I ask her and get back to ya."

"All right."

"Now, let me go find Timmy and have him fetch that insulation."

When Betty returned, she rang up his purchase, then handed him the receipt after he paid. "Since you'll be around for the festival, you ought to stop by the church. We put on our own little art fair and Irish stew dinner. We feature a lot of local artists and we always have a good crowd. My daughter has a booth. She sells embroidered dish towels. Has her own business. She's single, you know. Name's Ellen. Just broke up with her boyfriend."

"I think you might have mentioned that last time I was in here," Rourke said, forcing a smile. "Hey, if I knew an artist who wanted to display, what would I need to do to get a booth for the art fair?"

"Talk to Father John. He's in charge of all of that. If there's space, he'll find it for you. Now, if you'll just pull around to the back, Timmy can load up your truck."

"Thanks," Rourke said.

As he wandered outside, a plan began to formulate in his head. Annie wouldn't have to go to a gallery or a gift shop. She could sell her art at the festival. She could price each item and he could help her man the booth. And whatever she made could help play for some of the things she needed done around the cottage.

He pulled around to the back of the hardware store and found Timmy Bryant standing on the loading dock. Timmy, a high school senior, had worked for Rourke at Buddy's place for ten dollars an hour when Rourke needed an extra pair of hands. They'd become pretty good friends, talking about sports and women, higher education and life on the island. Timmy was planning to become a veterinarian and was headed to school in Montreal in the fall.

"Hey, there," Timmy said with a wide grin. "I heard you decided to hang around a little longer."

"Oh, yeah? Who'd you hear that from?" Rourke teased.

Timmy shrugged. "Oh, it's been around town.

People are saying you're staying out at the Macintosh place. How's that goin' for ya?"

"None of your goddamn business," Rourke said, chuckling to himself.

"Well, just be careful. You know what they say about Annie Macintosh."

Rourke grabbed the roll of insulation from Timmy's hands. "No, what do they say?"

Timmy frowned, then shook his head. "Nothin'. They don't say anything."

"Tell me. What do they say about her?"

The kid stared down at his feet, looking as if he wanted to crawl into the nearest hole. "They say she's a—a siren. Like her mama."

Rourke blinked in surprise, startled by the revelation. "They don't know what the hell they're talking about."

"No, not that kind of siren. The other kind. The one that sits on the rocks and lures men into their watery graves. You know, like from the myths."

"I know what a siren is," Rourke said.

"Just be careful," Timmy warned. "You don't want her to do to you what her mama did to her father. He drowned, you know. Heard her singing and walked right out into the North Atlantic to find her."

"It's a pretty story," Rourke said, "but I can assure you that Annie Macintosh is just an ordinary woman."

"That's how they disguise themselves," Timmy said. "So you don't see it comin'."

The teenager tossed the last roll of insulation into the SUV, then stuffed his hands into his jeans pockets. "I guess that's all."

"If you hear that story again, you just let whoever is spreading it know that it's not true. Take it from me. Almost all of what you hear about Annie Macintosh is probably rumor and conjecture."

"Rumor and conjecture," Timmy repeated. "Right. I'll remember that. And hey, if you need any help, you have my number. I still gotta make more money for university."

"I'll see what I can find," Rourke said. "Take care now."

He hopped into the front seat of the truck and turned the ignition, then slowly pulled away from the loading dock. As he headed out of town, he took the opportunity to consider Timmy's warning. It was ridiculous that they thought Annie possessed the power to drive him to his death. It was about time that the town of Pearson Bay got to know the real Annie Macintosh and he had the perfect way to make it happen.

ANNIE HEARD THE sound of Rourke's truck from inside the cottage. She wiped her hands on the dish towel, then grabbed her jacket and headed outside. He'd mentioned that he was going to the hardware store and she'd assumed it was for the insulation for her attic. But she hadn't expected him back quite so quickly. He'd barely had enough time to get halfway to town.

As she rounded the corner of the house, she saw Sam Decker's police cruiser. The police vehicles on the island were sturdy SUVs, equipped with the flashing lights and the official emblem of the Cape Breton Regional Police Service on the side.

Annie hesitated, wondering if he'd seen her yet. Maybe she could still make a run for it. But he waved at her, then jumped out of the truck. She groaned inwardly. The last thing she wanted to do was continue the conversation they'd started in front of the restaurant last night.

"Hi, Sam. How's it going?"

"Good as can be expected. We're gearing up for Celtic Colors. That starts on Friday. Lots of tourists coming to the island. Are you planning on going to see any of the concerts? I could get you tickets if you want."

Annie smiled gratefully, then shook her head. "I'm not one for crowds." She paused. "Why are you here, Sam?"

An angry expression came across his face. "Why is *he* here? What does Quinn have that I don't? Damn it, Annie, you know how I feel about you. I've been patient, thinkin' this was just going to take a little more time, but now I'm thinkin' it's never going to happen."

"I don't think it will," she murmured.

"Well, now's a fine time to tell me, after I wasted the past three years thinkin' you were the one."

Annie shook her head. "I never gave you any encouragement."

"You never discouraged me, either. What is it about him? Is it 'cause he's from the city and I'm just a local? That doesn't make him any better than me. I love you, Annie. I know I've never said it, but I do and I—"

Annie quickly reached out and pressed her fingertips to Sam's lips. "Don't. Don't say any more. It's not going to make a difference. You know why this will never work. I told you why."

"Geez, Annie, we were kids. And I was just actin' stupid like kids do."

"You tormented me for almost six years. How am I supposed to forget that? Or trust that anything you say to me is real?"

"I did what I did because I liked you. I just didn't know how to show you."

"No," Annie said, shaking her head. "You did what you did because it made you feel powerful. It made you look good to your friends."

"I've apologized," he said. "What else do you want from me? I'll do whatever you ask."

Annie gave him an apologetic shrug. "Forget about me," she said. "That's what I want you to do."

He stared at her, speechless, then turned and walked back to his truck. Annie felt tears flooding the corners of her eyes. After all the torture she'd endured at his hands, she still regretted hurting him. Yes, he'd apologized and more than once. And she'd forgiven him. But there was just something inside her that couldn't forget.

As Sam drove way, she saw Rourke pass him on the narrow driveway. Annie groaned inwardly, knowing that there would be questions to answer. Since the woodpile wasn't any larger, she wouldn't have that to fall back upon. Now that she thought about it, she'd probably have to find a new source for firewood. That might be a problem with the coming winter, especially without the money to pay for it.

Yet, even though she knew Rourke would not be pleased with Sam's visit, she also knew that he would figure out the firewood problem. He was a resourceful man, a man used to taking on a crisis with a calm head and a steady hand.

He pulled the truck up beside the cottage and hopped out, then strode to the end of the porch. "Hey there, sleepyhead. I'm surprised to find you up."

"I had a visitor," Annie said.

"I can see that. What did Decker want?"

"Nothing," she lied. "He just wanted to check up on me."

"Check up on me is more likely."

"He has a little bit of a crush," Annie admitted.

Rourke's gaze met hers and for a fleeting moment, it felt as if he could see directly into her soul. "Maybe you ought to give him a second look. He's got a steady job, he lives on the island. He's got qualities."

Annie smiled. "You have qualities, too." She paused. "Actually, he did let me know that he's not going to be bringing me firewood anymore."

"Hmm. No free firewood."

"It wasn't free. I traded for it."

"Well, this comes at an interesting time. I was just thinking on the drive back how you might be able to make a little money for yourself."

Until now, Annie hadn't been interested in money. Her life had been in perfect balance. But now, without firewood, things could go terribly awry. "And how is that?"

Rourke circled the porch and climbed the steps, then strode to her and grabbed her hand. "Come with me."

She followed him into the house and then through the door to the front parlor. With the shutters open, natural light flowed into the room. The chill of the nor'easter no longer hung in the air. In fact, the room was pleasantly warm.

"This is your money," he said. "Look at all of this." He reached down and picked up a box of intricately stitched quilt squares. "You could frame these and they'd sell for thirty or forty dollars. And those wildflower watercolors? Twice that."

"No," Annie said. "This is just…it's a hobby. I'm not that good."

"Decker's mom sells your paintings in her shop."

"Yeah, but she doesn't get anything for them."

"I stopped in her shop. She has a three-hundred-dollar price tag on a painting of the Louisburg light."

Annie gasped. "Three hundred? Really?"

"Really," he said. "And these copper Celtic crosses. They are exactly what people visiting the island for the festival are going to want to buy. I think you could get at least sixty or maybe seventy for one of these."

As he walked around the room, Annie began to realize that he was a little too familiar with the contents of her "warehouse." Had he been in here snooping? She felt her temper rise, then pushed her irritation aside. Rourke was trying to help her. Maybe it was time she showed a bit of gratitude.

"How would I do this? I mean, don't I need a shop or something?"

Rourke turned and grinned at her. “I’m glad you asked. Because I have a pretty good plan. You’ll start by selling at the St. Patrick’s Art Fair. I talked to Father John and he’s agreed to give you a table. We need to get some kind of tent to protect your work if it rains and I’ll have to build you something so you can display the bigger pieces. And we’ll have to get some of these framed and matted. I can make you some frames and cut some glass, but you’re going to have to take care of the—”

“Wait!” Annie cried. All of a sudden this was turning into a very complex operation. “Are you thinking that I’m going to go into town and sell this stuff?”

“Of course. That’s the whole point. People want to meet the artist and talk to you. They want to hear about your work. That’s what an art fair is all about.”

“No,” Annie said, fear bubbling up inside of her. “I can’t do that. Not in Pearson Bay. Maybe somewhere else, but not in Pearson Bay.”

“All right. But you’ll have to find another art fair. Maybe you can hop on the internet and—oh, no, you don’t have a computer. Or maybe you could call a few—wait, do you even have a functioning phone right now?” Rourke shrugged. “I’ve done my part. If you don’t want to take it the rest of the way, that’s up to you. Now, I need to get started on the attic.”

He left Annie standing in the middle of the parlor, surrounded by years and years of her work. Her art had always been a way to pass the time. When she completed a piece she really liked, it gave her a boost of confidence, a feeling of satisfaction. She'd never even considered turning her art into a business.

"Three hundred dollars," she murmured.

Maybe Rourke was right. Maybe this was the solution to her firewood problem. Maybe this could give her a little financial security. She could put something away for a rainy day.

Annie bent down and picked up a box of pen-and-ink greeting cards she'd drawn a few years ago. Tied up with a pretty satin ribbon, even these could fetch five dollars. She straightened and slowly took in the contents of the room. Selling her art would be no problem. She had no strong emotional attachment to any of this. But selling herself was an entirely different matter.

6

ROURKE SET UP a workshop on the ground floor of the lighthouse, spreading out his tools where he could find them quickly. It was the perfect place with plenty of room for supplies.

It hadn't taken Annie long to get on board. After all, she was a practical girl and she knew when it was time to come out fighting. She still worried over the social aspect of the art fair, but they'd been practicing a sales pitch in the evenings before bed and she seemed to be gaining a little more confidence.

Unfortunately, Rourke couldn't control the reaction of the townsfolk of Pearson Bay. They all had their own ideas about Annie and her family. Timmy's ridiculous rant about sea sirens was a perfect example. If that's what she was up against, then this might be much more difficult than he could predict.

The sound of a cell phone echoed through the lighthouse. Rourke had plugged in his cell phone for the first time since leaving Buddy's place and he hadn't missed it. He grabbed his phone to find a text from his friend who was subletting his apartment.

Pkg came today via mssngr. Looks imprtnt. Do?

Rourke dialed his friend's number and a few seconds later, Kyle picked up. "Hey, there. I got your text. Who is the package from?"

"Looks like some lawyer. It's a Manhattan return address. I thought you were going to be back by the first of the month."

"No, I decided to stay a little longer. Open it up and see what's inside."

"Hang on."

Rourke waited, listening to the sounds on the other end of the line.

"Okay," Kyle said. "It is from some lawyer. Her name is Maria Cantwell from a firm by the name of Rogers, Frane and Cantori. And old girlfriend?"

"I've never dated a lawyer," Rourke said.

"Wait. It looks like someone left you some money."

Rourke frowned. "No way. Who's playing a prank on me?"

"Hey, it looks legit. Some woman named Aileen Quinn. Says here that she's your great-aunt. The sister of your grandfather Diarmuid Quinn. It says you need to contact them at—"

"Listen," Rourke interrupted. "Throw that into an envelope and send it up here. But first, text me the lawyer's name and number. I'll just call her and see what she has to say."

"You could be rich," Kyle said.

"Nah, these things never work out that way. She's probably left me some family teapot or maybe a vase. No one in the Quinn family ever had any sort of money."

"Your dad did," Kyle said.

"Yeah, and my mom got every cent of that. Hey, I don't mind. I'm learning to live a simpler life these days."

"When are you coming home?" Kyle asked.

"I don't know yet. Maybe not for a while. Maybe not ever."

"Right. I don't think you're cut out for island life, Quinn. Not enough action. I thought you said there wasn't a single beautiful woman on the whole island."

"I was wrong," Rourke said. "There is one." He paused. "Text me that name and number. Right now."

He hung up, then walked to the door and stepped out into the warm noonday sun. The weather had turned and they were enjoying almost summer-like temperatures. He sat down on the stoop and waited for the text to come through.

When he glanced up from the phone, he saw Annie approaching. She carried a blanket over her arm and a basket in her right hand. She wore a faded cotton dress that exposed her lithe limbs. Her feet were bare and her auburn hair shone in the sun.

"You are the most beautiful thing I've ever seen," he said when she came to a stop in front of him.

"You've said that so many times, I'm starting to believe it."

"Believe it," he said.

"Did you get a call?" she asked, nodding at the phone.

"No. It was nothing. What do you have in the basket?"

"Lunch," she said. "I thought we'd go down to the water and eat since it's so nice out. Have you seen Lady Gray today? She didn't come up to the cottage this morning. I wonder if she's gone."

Rourke stood up and took the basket from her hand. "Come on, let's go look for her." He laced his fingers through hers and they walked down to the shoreline.

The lighthouse was set on a rocky rise overlooking a small cove. The far shore of the cove was a low, craggy cliff, but the near shore had a small strip of sand. They headed down to the beach, Kit trotting along behind them.

When they reached the sand, Annie spread out the blanket. He set the basket in the center, then shrugged out of his shirt before he sat down. "This is nice," he said, holding his hand out to her.

Annie sank down beside him, then crawled onto his lap, straddling his hips. "Why don't you take off the rest of your clothes," she suggested.

"We're going to eat al fresco?"

She reached out and smoothed her hand along his jaw, then traced a path across his forehead with her fingertips. "You could kiss me now."

"I could do that," he murmured. Rourke brushed his lips against hers, his tongue gently tracing the crease of her lips. Annie sighed softly, then pulled him into another kiss. Her lips parted and he tasted fully, rolling her beneath him as the kiss deepened. Suddenly, he didn't really care about lunch.

He smoothed his hand along her thigh, moving beneath the soft fabric of her skirt. When he reached her backside, he realized that she was naked beneath the dress. His fingers moved to the buttons down the front and he worked them open one by one. Rourke cupped the soft flesh of her breast, then bent to tease her nipple with his tongue. She furrowed her fingers through his hair and drew him closer.

Though Rourke had hours of work to do before the festival, his attention was focused entirely on Annie. The physical connection between them was undeniable. They couldn't seem to get enough of each other. But the more time they spent together, the stronger their emotional bond was growing.

He felt it, this undeniable need to protect her. It was as if he were the only person in the world who could possibly make her happy. Their life together was simple, yet profoundly satisfying. And he was beginning to believe that what he was feeling was love.

Rourke Quinn was falling in love. He hadn't even known it was happening to him until it was too late. And now there was nothing he could do about it.

Annie reached down for the hem of her dress and wriggled out of it, lying on the blanket next to him. He took in the sight of her, her skin pale beneath the noonday sun.

Following her lead, Rourke skimmed his jeans over his hips and kicked off his boots. When he'd discarded the last of his clothes, he stretched out beside her. The sun felt glorious on his bare skin. His eyes drifted shut. They hadn't gotten much sleep the night before. Maybe a little nap before lunch was in order.

But a low bark from Kit brought him back to reality and he opened his eyes to find Annie's gaze fixed out on the water. Rourke pushed up on his elbow. "What is it?"

"Lady Gray," Annie said. She pointed to a spot in the middle of the cove. "See. There she is."

Annie scrambled to her feet and ran to the water's edge. He sat up and wrapped his arms around his knees, taking in the view. God, she was incredibly beautiful. He could count himself lucky that the only man on the island who'd noticed was Sam Decker. Any other place at any other time, Annie Macintosh would have been considered totally hot.

A few moments later, the seal was on the sand in front of her. She bent down and looked into the animal's eyes. For a long time, they just stared at each other. Then, with a throaty yelp, Lady Gray turned her head and waddled back into the water. She swam out to the entrance of the cove and popped her head out of the water once before she swam into the deeper water of the North Atlantic.

Rourke got to his feet and walked over to Annie. Wrapping his arms around her waist, he drew her back against his body. He pressed his lips to her shoulder.

"She won't be back," Annie said.

"Sure she will," Rourke said. "She'll come back next year."

"No. She won't come back. This was goodbye for good."

"Why do you think that?"

Annie shrugged. "I just know. I saw it in her eyes. We needed each other and now we don't."

Rourke stared at the horizon, hoping to catch another sight of the gray seal, but with the choppy water, it was impossible to see her.

"Can I tell you something and promise me you won't think I'm crazy?"

"I already think you're crazy," he teased.

"Crazier," she said.

"Tell me."

"I think Lady Gray is my mother. Reincarnated. Do you believe in reincarnation?" She turned in his embrace to look up at his face. "Does that sound silly?"

"No," Rourke said. "It doesn't sound silly at all."

"I found her on the rocks the day after my grandmother died. I was all alone and I was afraid and she was there. Something—or someone—to distract me from my troubles."

"Celtic mythology tells of selkies. Women who take the form of seals to enchant men."

"Maybe I just needed to feel that connection. I don't know. It's silly."

"We do what we have to do to get by," Rourke said. "There is something about that seal. I'm not sure what it is, but it's something."

Annie threw her arms around his neck and kissed him. "Thank you," she murmured.

"For what?"

"For being here. For listening to me. For helping me. You've done so much and I don't want you to think that I'm not grateful. I am. So grateful."

"Then feed me some lunch and make love to me on this beach," Rourke said.

"Do you want to take a swim first?" she asked. "The cove is pretty shallow, so the water will be warm enough." She took his hand and drew him toward the water's edge. "Come on, it will be fun."

Rourke had never swum naked before. And considering the invitation had been made by a very beautiful and very naked woman, he wasn't about to refuse. With a laugh, he reached down and scooped her up into his arms. "Come on, my little selkie. Show me your magical ways."

Annie screamed as he jogged into the water. When it was waist high, he lowered her from his arms and pulled her body against his. This day was perfect. This life was perfect. And he never wanted it to end.

ANNIE SAT ON the floor of the parlor, surrounded by her art, an unseasonably warm afternoon breeze blowing through the open windows. After breakfast that morning, Rourke had handed her a package of stickers and a marker and told her to price her artwork.

But after two hours of sitting and contemplating the value of her work, she hadn't managed to price a single piece. It wasn't that she couldn't decide what it was worth. She knew that once she put the first tag on, she was committed. Tomorrow night, she'd load her art into the back of Rourke's SUV and the next morning, they'd head into town to set up for the art fair.

She didn't want to back out now. After everything Rourke had done for her, making racks for her displays, driving all the way to Halifax to buy sheets of acetate to protect each piece. He'd also bought a simple mat cutter and a case of black matting, and she'd worked all day yesterday on matting her watercolors and her copper Celtic crosses.

All totaled, she had one hundred and thirty-two pieces she could sell—if she decided to sell at all. Annie inwardly chastised herself. What was wrong with her? How would Rourke feel if she backed out now? Could he really love a woman so cowardly, so insecure that she couldn't even attend an art fair?

She'd lived in her protective little cocoon for so long, she wasn't sure how she'd get along in social situations. Annie felt nervous in large crowds and she felt clumsy trying to make polite conversation. Had she been forced to learn these things as a child, she might not have such fears. But she couldn't help believing that everyone was judging her—and finding her severely lacking.

"Coward," she muttered to herself. "Coward, coward, coward."

Rourke believed she was strong and clever and resilient. She could do this if she just put her mind to it. She could.

Annie reached for one of her watercolors and stuck a small white tag on the upper right corner. What had Rourke told her they were worth? He'd been throwing out so many figures that night that she hadn't bothered to commit them to memory.

She looked down at the painting of a clump of wild violets and remembered when she'd painted it. It was the day she'd found Kit wandering in the woods. His fur had been matted and full of brambles and he'd been limping from a cut on his paw. He'd followed her home and she'd cleaned him up and fed him, then opened the door to send him on his way.

The next morning, he'd been waiting on her porch, and from that moment on, he'd taken up residence with her. She'd asked Sam to post a note with the local humane society about a lost border collie, but no one had called to claim him.

"That was a good day," she murmured.

"Are you almost done?"

Annie glanced over her shoulder to see Rourke standing in the doorway. He'd discarded his shirt and wore a pair of cargo pants that rode low on his hips, exposing the well-defined muscles of his abdomen. "I haven't started," she confessed.

"Why not?"

Annie shrugged. If he truly loved her, then he'd understand her fears. But there had been no real admissions of love between the two of them. Though their desire for each other hadn't cooled by even a single degree, they hadn't really defined the relationship they seemed to be enjoying.

Were they friends or lovers? Was this a vacation affair or the beginning of a lifelong partnership? Just how deep did his feelings go? Annie wanted—no, she needed—to know.

"I can't do this," she said. "I don't want to do this."

"What don't you want to do? Price your art?" Rourke asked, a suspicious glint in his gaze.

"All of it. Price my art, sell it at the art fair, try to act nice around people who think I'm weird. I don't want to do it."

He stared at her for a long moment, then shrugged. "Fine. If you're not ready, you're not ready. I'm sorry I pushed you."

With that, he turned around and walked out of the room. Annie got to her feet. That was far too easy. After all the planning he'd done, all the money he'd spent, he was just going to give up?

Maybe he'd stopped caring. Maybe he'd realized that she was a lost cause and that she'd never change. Why would a man like Rourke even bother with a girl like her? Pity only went so far, but now it was clear that he'd reached the end of his rope.

Annie strode out to the kitchen, ready to confront him, to demand that he be honest about his feelings for her. But he'd already gone back to the lighthouse, no doubt to set fire to everything he'd already built for her.

As she stepped to the door, she heard a musical sound. She turned to see Rourke's cell phone vibrating across the kitchen table. She walked over to grab it, then noticed the name on the screen. Maria Cantwell.

She hesitated, then picked the phone up and pressed the green button to receive the call.

"Hello?"

The voice on the other end greeted her. "Hello. Is Rourke there?"

"Not right now," she said.

"Can you tell him I called," she said. "Maria."

"Can I ask what—"

"Oh, he'll know. Don't worry. Just let him know I returned his call. Bye."

The woman clicked off on the other end. "Oh,

he'll know," Annie muttered. She'd never come right out and asked him if he had a girlfriend. She'd never asked him if he had a wife, either. Had she forgotten an important step here?

Annie groaned and sank onto a kitchen chair. She hadn't asked because she'd assumed he'd be honest when contemplating her offer of seduction. In truth, it was a perfect situation for an unhappily married man: a few nights of hot sex in a remote cottage with a willing partner. What man wouldn't have jumped at the chance?

She grabbed his phone and headed outside, then strode up the path to the lighthouse. When she reached the open door, she found Rourke inside, sweeping sawdust off the floor. He didn't look up at her and she could tell by his body language that he was holding his temper.

"You had a phone call. It was Maria. She said you'd know what it was about." Annie held out the phone and he took it from her and stuffed it in his pocket.

"Thanks," he murmured.

"I'm sorry," she said. "I want to do this. I'm just not sure I can."

He met her gaze. "You won't know until you try. I'll be there, just like I was that day when we were kids. If anyone causes you trouble, I'll be there."

"It—it just feels like...surrender," she said.

"Surrender? How?"

"I've been fighting them so long. Trying to keep them from hurting me. Refusing to play by their rules. And now I'm going to act like it never made any difference to me."

Rourke stepped in front of her and took her hands. "Do you trust me?" he asked.

Annie nodded. "I do."

"Then trust me on this. If I thought for even a moment that this would be bad for you, I'd never ask you to do it. Do you believe me?"

She wanted to believe him, but then there was Maria. Who was she and what did she mean to him? "The phone call," she said. "Is that your girlfriend?"

Rourke drew back, looking down at her with a wry smile on his face. "No."

She swallowed hard. "Please don't tell me she's your wife."

"That's a big no," he said. "I'm not married and I don't have a girlfriend."

"So I guess that also rules out a fiancée?"

"Maria is a lawyer. She's dealing with an inheritance."

"From Buddy?"

"No," he said. "From another relative I didn't know I had. I guess she's trying to figure out if I'm the guy she's looking for."

Annie felt a warm blush creep up her cheeks. "I thought maybe… I just never asked if you were involved, and now I am." She drew a ragged breath. "That's good then."

"So what about the art fair? Are you in or out? Because, if you're in, I need to finish this rack before the end of the day."

"I'm in," Annie said. "I'll do it."

He bent close and kissed her forehead. "I'm glad. You'll see, this will be good. You'll sell your art and make some money."

"And pay you back for everything you spent on materials," she added.

"We'll talk about that later."

"I am going to pay you back," Annie insisted.

"We're going to have to take these racks over today. I talked to Betty at the hardware store and she said we can store them on her loading dock until the morning of the show. We'll take all your stuff over and then I'll run and get the racks and we can set up. The show opens at ten, so we'll probably have to get to town by eight?"

"Right," she said. "That sounds good."

He pulled her into a fierce hug. "What do you say I finish up here and grab a shower and I'll take you out for dinner. We'll go into Pearson Bay. You can dip a toe before you jump in headfirst."

Annie had decided to put herself in his hands. If she freaked out, then that would be the end of it. But Rourke was right. She did owe it to him, and herself, to try. It wasn't really surrender. She wouldn't change to fit their idea of normal.

ROURKE ROLLED OVER in bed and reached out for Annie's warm body. But her side of the bed was cold and empty. He sat up and looked around the room. The weather had been so warm, they hadn't needed a fire and the only light came from the lamp on the kitchen table.

"Annie?" He swung his legs off the edge of the bed and stood. He didn't bother to grab any clothes and walked to the screen door. She sat on the top step staring out at the water. She was wrapped in an old afghan that usually hung over the back of the rocking chair. Kit was sitting beside her, his nose up, sniffing the breeze that blew off the ocean.

"What are you doing out here?" he asked.

"Thinking," she said.

"About what?"

She drew a deep breath and let it out slowly. "Everything is changing. I'm changing. I thought I understood what my life was and I was all right with it. I was happy. But now I have new things happening and I'm worried that it will make my old life seem…unsatisfying."

He took her hand and laced his fingers through hers. "What's wrong with that?"

"You'll go home, I'll go back to the way things were, and I'll be unhappy."

Rourke drew her hand to his lips and pressed a kiss below her wrist. "I've been thinking I might stay. I have Buddy's cottage and the land it's on. There's no reason for me to go right now."

"What about New York? Don't you miss your friends? Your family?"

"No," he said. "I'm really starting to enjoy this place. You. Us, together. What do you think?"

"I think you've known me for a week. It's a little too soon to change your whole life for someone you barely know."

"I know enough," Rourke said. He stood up and drew her to her feet. The afghan fell away from her naked breasts. "Come back to bed."

He pulled the door open and she stepped inside. As she crossed to the corner of the room, she let the afghan fall to the floor. Rourke's breath caught in his throat and he paused to watch her in the dim light from the lamp.

When she reached the bed, Annie turned and held out her hand to him. They sank onto the mattress together, their bodies already entwined in a familiar prelude to what they were about to do.

But this night was different. This night wasn't a crazy race to release. This was slow and sweet. He lingered over each caress, and her fingers and lips explored every inch of his body. Though he'd told her he was planning to move into Buddy's house, in truth, Rourke couldn't imagine spending a single night away from her.

It had been a week, but they'd lived a lifetime in those seven days. He'd never experienced anything like this with any other woman. And it wasn't just about sex. There was an undeniable bond between them, as if they were always meant to be together.

She made him slow down and enjoy the little things in life, the truly important things. And he was helping her conquer her past and face her future. Rourke wanted that future to include him, but he knew he'd have to wait.

It had taken a lot of effort to breach the walls she built around her. But she could throw them up a lot faster than he could knock them down. It was too soon to talk about a future together—for both of them.

He lost himself in the taste of her mouth, and rational thought slowly slipped from his mind. Annie rolled on top of him, her legs straddling his hips. She caught his hands above his head and leaned over him, her breasts brushing against his chest.

She teased him, smiling down at him, her hair wild around her face. This one thing would never change between them, he thought. This would always be perfect.

When she shifted above him, he held his breath, the tip of his shaft slipping into her damp heat. He waited for her to move again, to grab the box of condoms from the bedside table. But instead, she slowly took him inside her, inch by delicious inch, until he was completely buried.

Rourke wanted to stop her, wanted to remind her what they were risking. But he didn't care. If there were consequences to this night, it would link them forever. And wasn't that what he wanted?

She began to move, and Rourke watched her, her naked body flushed with passion. Her lip was caught between her teeth and her eyes fluttered. They'd learned each other's signs, the sighs and the gasps, the shifts in tempo that meant release was close at hand.

Usually they reached their orgasms together, but this time, Rourke wanted to watch her. He reached between them and touched her, his fingers sliding between her moist folds. She was so close to the edge that the momentary caress was all it took to bring on the shudders and spasms.

She arched against him, her hands splayed across his chest, her head tipped back. It took every last ounce of his self-control to wait until she was completely spent, and when she collapsed, he pulled her beneath him and drove into her just once.

He surrendered to the power of his orgasm. Pleasure pulsed through his body and he held on to her hips when she rocked against him. And when it was finally over, Rourke kissed her, tasting deep of her sweet mouth.

"Sometimes, I think I could spend the rest of my life in this bed and be perfectly happy."

"We have to go to the art fair in the morning," she said.

"I'm not making you go," he replied with a chuckle. "In fact, right about now, I'm thinking we should stay in bed."

"Really?"

She sounded so hopeful. Maybe he had been pushing too hard. He couldn't expect her to conquer all her fears in just one week. And though they'd had dinner in town that evening, he could tell she was a bundle of nerves throughout.

As she'd predicted, people had stared at them and whispered to each other, and no doubt there would be wild speculation over what was going on at Freer's Point.

"Yes, really," he said.

"But we did all that work."

"And now you're ready to go if you decide to go. Without doing all that, you wouldn't have been ready."

She pushed up on her elbow and smoothed her palm over his chest. "Do you think I need to see a psychiatrist?"

Rourke laughed. "What brought that on?"

"I've just been thinking that maybe…I mean,

I've read about people who are afraid of crowds or strangers or even leaving their houses."

"Agoraphobics," Rourke said. He had to admit that the thought had crossed his mind. But Annie's reluctance to socialize had more to do with stubbornness than fear. She stayed away to prove a point—that she didn't need anyone's help. Or pity.

But their time together had changed all that. She'd made it pretty clear that she wanted him—maybe even needed him just a bit. And she was learning that it wasn't a bad thing to have someone to depend upon. Someone she could trust.

"Do you think that's me?" she asked.

"No," Rourke replied. "I mean, I'm no shrink, but I believe that you're perfectly capable of doing anything you set your mind to. I think that you had a very sad childhood and you coped the only way you knew how. But that made you into a strong and resilient woman."

"I don't always feel strong," she said.

"Neither do I," Rourke said. "We all have our insecurities."

"You have insecurities?" Annie laughed. "Really? Name one."

"When I was a kid, I had really big ears. My dad always said I'd grow into them. My mom wanted me to go to a plastic surgeon and have them fixed. That's why I always wear my hair long. To cover up my ears."

Annie frowned, then reached up and brushed the hair away from his right ear. "I love your ears," she said. "I think they're perfect."

"And I love your mouth," Rourke said, pulling her into a kiss. "Your soft lips and your sweet tongue. And I love your nose and those freckles across the bridge. And your hair and your hands. I pretty much love every little part of you."

"I am going to go to the art fair," Annie said. "I'm ready to move on. It's time I start acting like a full grown woman instead of a scared kid."

"I don't have any doubts about the full grown woman thing," Rourke teased. "And I'm going to be right there, by your side."

It was a promise he was happy to give her for the next week. But he was beginning to believe that it might just be a promise that would last a lifetime.

7

THE OPENING DAY of the Celtic Colors music festival brought a crowd of tourists into Pearson Bay. There were concerts spread all over Cape Breton, in a variety of venues, and along with that, many of the small towns added events of their own, hoping to capitalize on the influx of people.

Though Annie had never been much for crowds, Rourke had set her up in the tent with a comfortable chair, a cooler full of snacks and a promise that she wouldn't have to talk to anyone if she didn't want to.

For the first hour, people mostly browsed, moving from tent to tent and taking in everything the art fair had to offer. But right before lunch, those same people started to buy. Annie watched as Rourke pointed the customers toward works they might enjoy. But he didn't know the stories behind her pieces and she thought it was important for the buyer to know everything about her art.

When he was trying to describe one of her embossed Celtic crosses, she grew impatient when he kept calling it an etching. Annie pushed out of her chair and stepped to his side, then patiently explained the technique she had used to get the detail embossed into the copper.

From then on, it seemed easier to talk to people. Most of the customers were tourists, but several citizens of Pearson Bay stopped by to say hello to Rourke and to nod at her. That didn't satisfy Rourke. He invited them to look at Annie's work, asking her to tell them about it.

"Well, Annie, it looks like your booth is one of our most popular."

Annie looked up from straightening her woodcut prints to find Father John grinning at her. "Thank you," she said, suddenly uneasy. Was he upset that she was stealing business from the other artists? "I mean, they've been looking."

"And buying," Rourke said. "It's going well."

Father John smiled. "Annie, I haven't seen you in church since we said our goodbyes to your grandmother. We've missed you. And I suspect that you've missed the church. And Rourke, once you move back to your uncle's place, we'd like to see you in our congregation."

His implication was clear. Father John obviously didn't approve of the two of them cohabitating. It had barely been two hours and already she was being judged. But then, wasn't that Father John's job?

"Have you seen Annie's Celtic crosses?" Rourke asked, deftly shifting the subject. "As a man of the cloth, I think you might need to have one of these."

Annie moved on to help another customer and to her delight, managed to make three sales in a matter of minutes. She glanced up at the crowd gathered around her tent and felt a bit giddy with all the excitement.

By two o'clock they'd sold at least twenty-five pieces and were holding another six or seven for customers who were going to stop back on their way out. Annie was hungry and thirsty and needed a bathroom break.

"I'm going to go get us some lunch," she said. "I smell hamburgers and I want one."

"Me, too," Rourke said. "Two. With ketchup, pickles and onions."

"No onions," she teased. "I don't want you driving away the customers." Annie leaned closer and brushed a kiss across his lips. "Thank you," she murmured.

"For what?"

"For this," she said. "For believing I could do this. You deserve a lot more than a kiss, but that will have to wait until later."

He grabbed her shoulder and gave her another quick kiss. "I can hardly wait."

Annie left the booth with a smile on her face and as she walked to the church and the public bathrooms, she was surprised by the number of people who smiled back at her as they passed. Everyone was in such a good mood.

By the time she reached the lunch tent, she was feeling almost euphoric. All of her fears had dissipated and she felt as if she could handle almost anything. Until she came face-to-face with Sam Decker.

"Annie," he said, the greeting coming out with a gasp. "I didn't expect to see you here."

After their last conversation, she wasn't sure they'd ever speak again. She'd been brutally honest with him and she knew she'd hurt him deeply. "Hi, Sam. How's it going?"

"Good. It's going good. It's—ah, good. Good to see you." He glanced down at his shoes, pushing a clod of grass around with his toe. "You look real pretty."

Annie couldn't help but smile. "Thank you," she said.

"Can I buy you lunch?" he asked, nodding at the food tent.

"Actually, I just came over to pick up something for Rourke and me. I have a booth here. Next to the guy with the stained glass. You should come over and see it. Maybe pick out a few things to take. I still owe you for the last cord of wood that you brought me."

"So he's still here. He's with you."

Annie wasn't sure how to answer that question. She and Rourke hadn't talked about what they had or didn't have together. She'd been quite content to take it day by day. But now they'd be forced to define their relationship so everyone else would be able to understand it.

"Yes, he's still here," she said softly.

Sam reached out and snatched her hand. She tried to pull away, but he held tight. "Someday, he's going to go back to wherever he came from, Annie. He doesn't belong on the island any more than you belong in a big city. And when he leaves, I want you to know that I'll be waiting. I'm willing to wait for you, Annie."

"Don't do that, Sam. Please, don't."

He forced a smile, then drew a deep, deliberate breath. "It's never going to happen, is it?"

"No," Annie said, the pain in his expression sending a dagger of guilt through her heart.

"No matter what I do or say?"

She shook her head. "No matter what you do or say. It's not that I don't care about you, Sam. You're my friend. And after all you've done for me, I wish I could love you. It's not your fault, it's mine."

"People can change, Annie. Maybe you can change, too?"

His words took her by surprise. He had changed. More than she ever thought he could. Why wasn't that possible for her? Why couldn't she learn to trust? Why couldn't she allow herself to love Rourke?

She glanced around, then tugged her fingers from his grasp. "I—I'll see you…later. Come by and pick out a painting before all the good ones are gone."

Sam nodded. "I'll do that."

Annie spun on her heel and hurried through the crowd. When she reached her tent, she found Rourke relaxing on the lawn chair, sipping a bottle of cold water. He smiled at her as she stepped behind the table. "I sold one of the oils," he said. "Three hundred dollars." He frowned. "No lunch?"

"The line was too long," Annie lied. "I'll go back again later." She leaned up against the edge of the table and watched him for a long moment. "Can I ask you a question?"

"Sure," he said. "The answer is yes. I do expect a commission from that sale. I'll take it in sexual favors."

"That wasn't my question," Annie said. "How would you describe our relationship? I mean, are you my friend? My boyfriend? Should I call you my lover? I need to know."

"Why?"

"So I know what to tell people when they ask."

"Who's asking?"

"I just ran into Sam. And I didn't know what to say to him. I think we might want to...define things."

"All right," he said slowly. "Well, I guess I am your friend. And I'm your lover. And your boyfriend. All three. How's that?"

Annie grinned at him, then nodded. "That's fine. You're my boyfriend." She giggled. "I've never had a boyfriend. That sounds kind of strange coming out of my mouth."

"Well, get used to it," Rourke warned. He stood up. "I'm going to go brave the lunch line and get my girlfriend a burger. What would you like on it?"

"Everything. And bring me two. I'm starving."

Annie watched him weave through the crowd, smiling to herself. "That's my boyfriend," she said.

"Excuse me, are you the artist Annie Macintosh?"

She turned to find an elderly man standing at her table. The question took her by surprise. She was now the girlfriend and the artist, all in one day. "I am," Annie said.

The man held out his hand. "I'm Franklin Phillips. I publish greeting cards. I've had a chance to look at your note cards. The pen-and-ink drawings of the forest animals?"

"I—I'm afraid someone has purchased those already," Annie said, glancing around the tables.

"My wife did. And she was crazy about them. I'd like to talk to you about publishing some of your art. We do posters and small prints and note cards and fine art calendars. A whole range of products. And we'd like to add you to our roster of artists."

Annie was stunned. And flattered. But this man had the wrong idea. "My art is just my hobby," she said. "Just something I do in my spare time."

He shrugged. "You're a talent. And I look for talent." Phillips pulled out a business card and held it out. "I know you're busy right now, but send some samples of your work to that email address and we'll talk. I hope to hear from you."

Annie stared down at the card, not sure what she should think. She should feel excited, but she felt scared. And a bit overwhelmed. Having an actual job with a boss meant responsibilities. Interactions and deadlines. And she really wasn't an artist, she just played at art. She was a good cook but no one was going to offer her a job as a chef, were they?

She tucked the card into her pocket. And how was she supposed to send him samples of her work? She didn't have email. She didn't even have a computer. And if she sold everything she had, there wouldn't be any work left. This was all so unnerving. Her life had been so simple just a week or two ago. And now it was becoming very complicated.

ROURKE STARED ACROSS the table at an exhausted Annie. They'd finished up the day at the art fair and packed up the few pieces that were left. He'd insisted that they go out for dinner to celebrate and they'd decided on a small café in Pearson Bay. He'd considered the day quite a victory, but now that he'd had a chance, Rourke could see what a toll this had all taken on her.

"I counted up the cash," he said. "Care to take a guess what you made?"

She sighed. "I—I don't know. A couple thousand?"

"Father John said your booth was one of the most popular. And even though you'll probably sell out before the weekend, he asked me to tell you about the church's Christmas craft fair. He hoped you might want to donate something they can raffle off."

"Sure," she said.

Rourke reached across the table and grabbed her hand, lacing her fingers through his. "Three thousand seven hundred and sixty. That's what you made."

Annie gasped. "Really?"

"Really," he said. "With the way that you can stretch a dollar, you could do a couple shows a year and have plenty to buy yourself some creature comforts."

She thought about it for a long moment. "I'll have enough to buy wood."

"That's all that you can imagine doing with your money?"

"Everything that you want me to do just costs more money in the end. If I get electricity in the cottage, I have an electrical bill every month. If I get heat, I have a propane bill. If I buy a car so I can get to art fairs, there's insurance and gas and upkeep. Things get much more complicated. There are so many obligations."

Rourke nodded. Somehow, he knew she was talking about more than just selling her artwork. Until now, her life had been self-contained. She didn't need anyone other than herself to survive. But the more she ventured away from the cottage, the more she'd come to depend on others. "I see your point. Isn't there something you really need?"

"I need to pay you for the roof and the insulation in the attic."

"All right. We can start there. And maybe, instead of your bike, we could buy you a scooter. The gas wouldn't be too much and—"

"I don't have a driver's license," Annie blurted out.

"Then a moped. I don't think you need a license for that. It would make your trip into town much easier and faster. And you wouldn't have to struggle against the wind that comes off the Atlantic."

"I suppose I could…" She met his gaze. "Can we go? I really want to go home."

"We just ordered." Rourke smiled. "I'll ask the waitress if we can get it to take away."

This brightened her expression. "Yes. Let's do that."

Rourke flagged down the waitress and made the request, then finished his beer. He saw Betty Gillies across the café and gave her a wave. To his surprise, she made a beeline for their table.

"Rourke!" she said. "And Annie."

"Hi, Betty," Rourke said.

"Hello," Annie murmured.

"I just had to come over and tell Annie how everyone is talking about her art. We never knew you had such talent."

"Thank you," she said.

"I do have a proposition for you. I'm vice president of the Cape Breton Bird-watchers Association and we do a yearly fund-raiser. We were wondering if you'd create some note cards for us. Of course, we'd pay you. And we'd get a printer to donate the printing. It would be a way to have your art seen by many people, both on and off the island."

Annie glanced over at Rourke. He could tell she wasn't sure what to say. But it was time for her to make her own decisions. "It sounds like a good idea."

"Yes," Annie said.

"Yes, it's a good idea?" Betty asked. "Or yes, you'll do it?"

"Both," Annie said, forcing a smile.

"All right then. We'll talk more the next time you stop by the hardware store. We'll need something by January. Not many summer birds to draw now. But we have many photos to share. Well, I'll let you get back to your meal. Thank you, Annie. We're very excited to find such a talent on the island."

Betty hurried out and a few seconds later, the waitress appeared, carrying their dinner in two paper bags. Rourke quickly paid the bill, then walked with Annie to the front door. When they got outside, he could see her relax. Her shoulders, once tense, now dropped, and she drew a deep breath of the cool night air.

"It's been quite a day," he said.

"I don't have many memories of my childhood, at least not memories that include my parents. But I do remember one thing very well. They took me to a carnival one summer. I must have been four or five. It was before my mother got really…sick. And the three of us went on a Ferris wheel. I sat between them and we went up so high and they were both laughing. I was happy and scared all at once. We were so far off the ground and I thought we might fall. But I was tucked in between them and they were keeping me safe. I knew there was something going on between them. They fought a lot and my mother would take to her bed for days. But for that one day, we were all so happy."

"And what brought that memory back?" Rourke asked.

"I felt the same way today. I was happy, but scared at the same time. I felt sick to my stomach and giddy. People believe I'm an artist and—"

"You *are* an artist," Rourke insisted.

"And I felt afraid because things are changing so quickly. I'm not sure who I am anymore."

"That's the way life is, Annie. Your life has been on hold for a while. But now it's moving forward. You don't need to be afraid. I'm here. I'll help you."

"I should be able to do this myself," Annie replied. Would she ever trust anyone enough to accept help, even as something as simple as moral support?

"Yes, you should," he said. "But I feel somewhat responsible since I started you down this road."

She stopped on the sidewalk and turned to him. "Do you really think you're going to stay on Cape Breton?"

Rourke reached out and cupped her cheek in his palm. He leaned close, brushing a kiss across her soft lips. "More and more, I think this might be the life for me."

"And you'll just walk away from your life in New York? And you won't miss it?"

"There are things I'll miss," he said. "Things I can't get here."

"Like what," Annie asked.

"A giant slice of pizza. A decent hot dog. Onion bagels and the *Sunday Times*. A bookstore with every kind of book I could possibly want. Movie houses that show obscure foreign films. And a few other things."

"If you'll miss that much, why would you want to move?"

"Because there is one thing on Cape Breton that I can't possibly find in New York."

"Your uncle's cottage?"

Rourke chuckled. "I was going to say you. You're here."

"Me?"

He grabbed her hand and started down the street again. "I thought we'd decided that I was your boyfriend. I know I'm your lover. And I'm thinking, I might want to be more."

"No," Annie said, shaking her head. "I—I didn't mean I thought you were my boyfriend. I just was afraid people would ask questions and I wouldn't know how to answer them."

Rourke frowned. Had he misunderstood? "I thought you were talking about your feelings for me."

"No. We had an agreement. This was just about sex. I can't— I mean, I'm not interested in anything else. I thought you understood that."

He didn't believe what he was hearing. There was no way she wasn't feeling the same deep, deep connection that he felt. They were more than just intimate strangers. But when he tried to force her to admit it, she put up the same old walls. He knew that pushing her into saying something she wasn't ready to give voice to would only make Annie push back even harder.

"Of course," he said. "You're right. We should keep this simple. Sex. Nothing more. I think some people would call it 'friends with benefits.' Are we at least friends?"

"Yes, we're friends."

Rourke bit back a curse. Would it always be this way with Annie? One step forward and two steps back. Or three—or four? She was the most confounding woman he'd ever met. He knew she felt something deeper than just a physical attraction. He'd be willing to bet his life on it. But there was something still holding her back. It wasn't trust, because he was sure that she trusted him. Though his patience could be stretched thin, sooner or later he'd figure her out. And then maybe they'd be able to talk about a future together.

ANNIE STARED AT the ceiling above the bed. The room was dark, with low light provided by the dying embers of a fire that Rourke had built when they got home.

The day had been exhausting but in a good way. Though it had all been too much to take in in such a short time, now that she had a chance to reflect, the positives far outweighed the negatives. She'd always considered her art something she'd done to please herself. But there had been people who were truly pleased to buy something she'd created.

They'd take her work and hang it in their homes or their offices. Or maybe they'd give it to someone as a gift. Whatever happened, their purchase was a tremendous compliment. But focusing on the positive only went so far. There was the other concern that had been keeping sleep at bay.

He was falling in love with her. Annie could see it in his eyes, in his smile. The way he'd touched her when they made love earlier had been different than before. And it wasn't just him, Annie thought. She was different, too.

In the beginning, it was all about physical pleasure, and they'd been good at providing that to each other. But now there was emotion behind what they did in bed.

Need was no longer the only thing that drove her into his arms. She felt safe and comfortable, valued, understood. Annie had never been able to trust, not completely. But with Rourke, she did.

And yet, one fear kept creeping in to spoil her happiness. She'd never worried about it before with men, but then none of those men had any intention of becoming a permanent part of her life.

She'd tried to convince herself that the fear was irrational, but then, irrationality would be one of the symptoms. Her mother had it and Annie was afraid that someday, she'd suffer the same affliction.

She'd heard the whispers in town, she'd read books and magazines about the illness, and she knew what they all thought—that Annie had inherited the disease from her mother. It was possible, she knew. Bipolar disorder could be passed along from generation to generation.

She'd seen what her mother's illness had done to her father and how it had affected her as a child. Annie didn't want that to happen to the family she might have. As much as she wanted a future with Rourke, would happiness elude them, as well?

She cursed to herself. Was this the way she wanted to live her life, just waiting for the other shoe to drop? What if she let Rourke wander out of her life and then twenty or thirty years later realized that there was no reason—that she'd lost her one and only chance at love simply because she was afraid?

Did her mother know it was happening to her, did she realize she was drifting out of control? Had she wanted to be "normal"? Or was she content with her life as it was? Annie had always believed that she was unaware. She wouldn't have willingly walked into the ocean and left her husband and daughter behind.

But if her mother had been unaware of the depth of her troubles, maybe Annie would be, too, if and when they came along. She gently pulled the covers back and slipped out of bed. The sun would be up in an hour. Grabbing the afghan from the back of her chair, she wrapped it around her naked body and walked to the kitchen door.

The sky to the east had already turned from inky black to deep blue and the stars had begun to fade. The moment she touched the doorknob, Kit leaped up from his spot near the fireplace and trotted to the door. They both slipped outside, into the cool of early morning.

Annie wandered down the path to the shore, Kit running out ahead of her, sniffing the air. He suddenly veered off the path and headed toward the lighthouse. The beam swept across the water and she stared up and watched as clouds raced through the predawn sky. Another storm was in the air. They'd have rain soon and then it would turn cold again. Unlike the rest of the islanders, she didn't need to listen to the weather forecast to know what was coming. She could feel it and smell it.

Annie walked out to the rocks and found a spot, perching on the flat surface of her favorite boulder. The sun had warmed the rock during the day and it still radiated heat, providing a sort of protection from the breeze off the water.

Kit leaped up beside her and she pulled him across her lap and nuzzled her face into the dog's fur. "Everything's changing," she whispered. "What do you think I should do?"

The dog wriggled in her lap and tried to lick her cheek. Annie laughed softly. "I remember when you were the only boy who kissed me. Now I've got a real boyfriend and I think he loves me." She rubbed the dog's belly. "Do you believe that?"

So if that was true, then what came next? Annie wondered. Would he admit his feelings out loud and would she then have to reciprocate? She let the words run through her mind before they formed on her lips. "I love you," she said, the sound disappearing in the breeze. "I love you."

She'd never said it to a single human being. She couldn't recall saying it as a child to her parents, and her grandmother had never been one to express her feelings. And the men in her life had never needed or wanted to hear the words.

"I love you," Annie said.

Maybe she was crazy, she thought. It was the only way to describe her behavior. She'd known Rourke for just over a week. Eight days. No one fell in love that fast, especially someone like her.

Annie sat on the rock until the dawn was just beginning to break on the eastern horizon. She was cold and confused, unsure of what would come next. They'd tried to be honest with each other, even when it wasn't easy. But Annie wasn't sure she could tell Rourke about this particular insecurity.

If she were a more selfish person, she might just forget the worry altogether and take her chances. But she did trust Rourke and if he truly loved her, like her father loved her mother, then what she feared about herself shouldn't make a difference.

When she reached the cottage, she silently slipped back inside, shushing Kit, who was anxious for his breakfast. Dropping the afghan on the floor beside the bed, she crawled back beneath the covers. Rourke stirred and then reached out and pulled her body into his.

"Why are you so cold?" he murmured, pressing his face into the curve of her neck.

"I was out watching the sun come up."

"Why didn't you wake me? I would have gone out with you."

"I wanted to be alone. I needed to think about some things."

"Am I included in those things?" he asked.

Annie shook her head. "No," she lied. She'd tell him the truth later, when she was ready to admit her fears. He deserved to know. Right now, she wanted to enjoy his warmth and maybe fall asleep for a bit.

"We don't have to go back to the art fair today," Rourke said. "You've sold almost all your work. Returning is hardly worth it. I'm thinking we should just spend the day at home."

"There's a small apple grove on my property," Annie said. "I usually go pick apples and then make applesauce. I could probably do twice as much if I had another pair of hands."

"I could help," he said. "As long as we get to spend the morning in bed, you have me at your beck and call for the rest of the day."

Annie yawned, her tired eyes watering. "I just need to sleep now," she murmured.

It was odd how everything seemed to be perfect as long as they stayed in bed. Without the outside world, there were no disagreements or disappointments. They could just focus on each other and not on the rest of the world. Annie was perfectly happy with Rourke, all alone.

But Rourke preferred to live in the real world, not in some sexual fantasyland inside her cottage. And if she wanted him in her world, she'd have to learn to live in his. But was his world here, on this island, or was it back in New York?

8

IT HAD BEEN a week since the art fair and Rourke hadn't made any moves to leave the island. In truth, he'd all but decided to stay. He had numerous messages on his cell phone, but he'd been ignoring them. And the phone had been buzzing all morning, but he hadn't picked up. There were two calls from the estate lawyer, Maria, three calls from his mother and another from one of his father's business partners.

Rourke was tempted to find out just what Ed Kopitski wanted, but he was afraid he wouldn't be able to hold his tongue. Even after all this time, his departure still stung. He'd invested almost eight years of his life with that firm, trying to replace his father and preserve his legacy.

But the partners, both old friends of his father, had insisted that they knew better how to run the firm and customers had gradually begun to fall away. By the time he'd gone, they'd barely been able to make payroll.

Did he really want to open that door again? He'd put that part of his life behind him and moved on to something new. And yet, the pull of his old life was still strong. Maybe Ed was willing to admit that he'd been right all along. That would be worth hearing, just for the sheer satisfaction of it.

"Are you ready to go?" Annie asked, stepping out onto the porch.

Rourke shoved his phone into his jacket pocket. "Yeah, let's go."

He and Annie had planned a drive over to his uncle Buddy's place. The folks who'd rented it for the festival had left the day before and he'd wanted to clean up before any prospective buyers came through.

The prospect of selling Buddy's place seemed more and more remote. Even if he got a great offer tomorrow, Rourke was sure he'd turn it down. Why not just take the place off the market? He'd need a place to stay if Annie didn't want him to move into the light keeper's cottage permanently.

"Thanks for helping out," Rourke said as they walked to his SUV.

Annie laughed. "Are you kidding? With everything you've done for me, I could at least scrub a few sinks and sweep a few floors."

"You do know that you'll be forced to use electrical appliances. A vacuum cleaner? A clothes dryer? Are you prepared for that?"

She gave him a playful punch on the shoulder. "Very funny. I'm sure I can manage."

They spent the drive over to Buddy's place chatting about the new art project she had started the night before. She'd decided to take up the birdwatchers on their offer and planned to show them twelve different illustrations to choose from. Rourke could see the excitement in her eyes as she explained how they could make two different sets of note cards and sell twice as many.

He couldn't help but take pride in her accomplishments. It was an odd feeling to be so invested in someone else's life, but there it was.

After passing through Pearson Bay, she fell silent. Rourke wasn't sure what was going through her head, but she had something she wanted to discuss. He could see it in her expression. Were they going to go over all that relationship stuff again? Was he her boyfriend or her lover? Right now, Rourke really didn't care what he was called. He was just happy to be with her.

"Here, look at this," Annie finally said.

He glanced over to find her holding a business card. "What's that?"

"Look at it."

"Franklin Phillips. Gray Goose Graphics and Printing. Halifax."

"He talked to me at the art fair. He wants to publish my note cards, too. And maybe some of my other work. He would pay me for my art."

"Of course he would pay you," Rourke said. "Annie, this is wonderful. This would be a regular income, something you could depend upon."

"I know."

"What did you say to him?"

"Nothing. I was just so shocked and a little confused."

"And why did it take you so long to tell me about it?"

"Because I wasn't sure what I wanted to do about it. And now I am. I want to do it. But I need your help."

"Sure," Rourke said. "Anything."

"He wants me to send samples of my work to him by email. And I'm not really sure how to do that since I don't own a computer. Do you know how to do that?"

"Well, first we'd have to take scans or digital photos of your work, then download them onto my laptop and then—"

"See. I don't really understand any of that. I'm not sure I want to. It sounds very complicated."

"It really isn't. It's actually quite easy and—"

"Just tell me the first part. One step at a time."

"All right. First you need to select some of your pieces that you think are representative of your best work."

"I sold all my best work."

"Then you need to go back and do more. Some of your paintings belong to people in town. We could ask to take photos of them. I'm sure they wouldn't mind. And you really only need one sample of each type of thing you've done."

"I'm not sure I can produce good work on demand."

"You'll do your best and see what happens."

He pulled into the driveway of the cottage, then steered the SUV up the small rise to the house. Annie stared out the window. Buddy's cottage looked much different than it had when she'd last seen it.

"Wow," she murmured. "It's like a bright new penny, all shiny and nice." She turned to him. "I like the color."

Rourke grinned. "Good. Come on, I'll show you around the place. You can see a sample of my work."

As he gave Annie the ten-cent tour, Rourke realized how much he'd enjoyed bringing the house back from ruin. It was now a comfortable and modern home, yet still retained all the charm of the past. As they walked into each room, Annie flipped on the lights, as if amazed at the convenience of having electricity at her command.

She found the gas fireplace particularly fascinating. "It looks like real wood," she said. "But it doesn't smell like it."

"I know. I could always change to a wood-burner if I wanted to. I really like the hearth at your place."

Rourke's phone rang and he glanced at the screen. It was his mother. She'd called three times in the past week and he hadn't called her back. "Why don't you look around upstairs. I just have to take this. It's my mother."

"Sure," she said. "I'm going to go check out the bedrooms."

He watched as she walked up the stairs, and then quickly dialed his mother. As usual, she answered on the seventh ring.

"Hello, Mom."

"Rourke! I was beginning to think you'd fallen off the planet. I thought you were headed home. Where are you?"

"I'm still on Cape Breton," Rourke replied. "Is everything all right?"

"Yes, of course it is. Why are you calling?"

"You called me, Mom. Three times."

"Oh, that's right. Well, I'm glad you called back. I just wanted to tell you to get in touch with Ed Kopitski. He's been calling here, asking if I'd pass along a message, and I just told him to call you directly."

"What message?" Rourke asked.

"They want you back at the firm. It seems they've run things into the ground and feel that only the son of the founder could get the company back on track. And of course, they're interested in your money."

"What money?"

"The inheritance from your great-aunt Aileen. I understand it could be almost a million dollars."

"A—a million?" Though Rourke had talked to the lawyer about the inheritance, she'd never brought up an amount and he hadn't bothered to ask. "Are you sure?"

"Yes. The investigator tracked me down and I gave him your number. But he said Aileen Quinn was prepared to leave you a million dollars. He said there were some conditions, but for a million dollars, I'd—"

"Stop saying a million dollars," Rourke snapped. "So, I'd assume that you told Ed about the money."

"Yes. It did come up in conversation. If you want my advice, let them go down in flames. They never appreciated what your father did for that business and they never appreciated you. Spend your money on something that makes you happy."

"Thanks, Mom."

"When are you coming home?"

"Soon. I think I'm going to have to come back to take care of this inheritance thing. I'll call you before I leave."

"Rourke? I'm really happy for you. I know you've been at loose ends since you quit. But now you have choices."

He hung up the phone, then immediately dialed Maria's number. When she picked up the phone, he couldn't help himself. "A million dollars? Why didn't you tell me we were talking about a million dollars?"

"Mr. Quinn?"

"Rourke," he said.

"Rourke. We usually don't like to discuss these things over the phone. Sometimes heirs spend the money as soon as they hear the amount, and before they learn the conditions."

"Which are?"

"I think it would be best if we talk in person," Maria said. "Can you stop by the office?"

"I'm not in New York. But I can be. Give me a couple days. I'll call you when I get into town." He drew a deep breath. "This woman is really giving me a million dollars?"

"She seems to be," Maria said. "She's searching out all the descendants of her brothers. You're not the only one who is benefiting from her generosity."

"Where did she get all this money?"

"She's Aileen Quinn. The Irish novelist?"

"Right," Rourke said. He didn't recognize the name, but he was going to look her up at the first available opportunity.

Rourke hung up the phone and then dropped it in his jacket pocket. He sat down on the sofa and thought about what had just transpired. He was about to be handed an incredible gift. For a guy who had been unemployed just yesterday, he now had prospects. He could do a lot with a million dollars. He could start his own business. He could travel the world for a few years. He could build a beautiful house here on the island.

He could afford to wait for Annie to fall in love with him. Though he'd thought about staying in Buddy's place, Rourke knew that he couldn't keep the house for long, not without a job. And finding any job on Cape Breton was going to be tricky. But now, he didn't need a job. With a million dollars, he'd consider himself independently wealthy.

He slowly stood. There were so many things to think about. Until he'd made some decisions, he wouldn't tell Annie about his windfall. She scraped by on three hundred dollars a month. How would she react when she found out he might become a millionaire?

Rourke climbed the stairs, expecting to find her in one of the bedrooms. But as he stepped into the hall, he heard running water in the bathroom. Curious, he pushed open the door only to find her naked, immersed in a tub full of hot water and bubbles.

"What are you doing?" he asked.

"Taking a bubble bath," she said. "Your guests left a bottle of shampoo. It makes nice bubbles. And they smell good."

His gaze drifted down the length of her body and he fought the urge to reach out and brush the bubbles away from her breasts. Rourke shrugged out of his jacket. When he'd put in the oversize whirlpool tub, he'd though it would increase the value of the house. He never thought he'd be using it for seduction.

"You know, that tub is made for two." He tugged his shirt over his head, not bothering with the buttons. His T-shirt followed, tossed to the floor onto a growing pile of clothes.

"Slow down," Annie teased. "I want to watch."

A naughty grin curled her lips as he finished his task. And when he was completely naked, she demanded that he turn around, offering her a view of the other side.

"All right," she said. "I guess you'll do."

Rourke turned to face her. "I'll do?" He stepped into the tub and sank into the warm water. "I'll do whatever you want me to do." He slipped his hand between her legs and found the spot that always drove her wild with passion.

"And after I'm done showing you the tub," he murmured, his mouth hovering over hers, "I think we ought to see the shower."

"WHAT DO YOU mean you're leaving?" Annie demanded. "When? Where are you going? Why?"

"I have to go to New York to settle some business. I'm not going to be gone long. No more than a week."

The news hit Annie like a sack of bricks. Though she'd always known there was a chance he'd leave, things had been moving toward Rourke's taking up residence on the island. He'd even taken Buddy's house off the market.

"You could come with me," Rourke said.

Annie shook her head. There was that strange feeling again—giddiness mixed with sheer terror. "No. That's not possible. I have a lot of work to do. I have to get things ready to send to Mr. Phillips. And—and there's Kit. Who would take care of him?"

"You can bring your work with you and we'll take Kit along, too."

"He's never ridden in a car. What if he doesn't like it?"

"Let's take him for a ride and see. Get your jacket." Rourke whistled to the dog, who was sleeping next to the bed. The border collie's ears perked up. "Come on, boy, you want to go for a ride?"

The words seemed familiar to the dog, who leaped to his feet and ran to the door, his tail wagging. Annie watched the two of them. Kit's loyalty had always been to her, but now he seemed just as anxious to please Rourke. "Maybe he would like the car. But where would we stay? Would there be a place for him to run? Is there grass in New York City?"

"We have a really big plot of grass. It's called Central Park."

Annie sighed. "I know about Central Park," she muttered. "How far do you live from the park?"

"Just a few blocks."

"So if he wants to go out at night, we have to put a leash on him and walk him two blocks to the park? That doesn't seem very practical."

"Is this really about Kit? Or is this about you?" Rourke asked.

His question stung and she knew she was being childish. If she really wanted a relationship with Rourke, she'd have to learn to conquer her insecurities. They couldn't stay on the island forever. There would be vacations and trips to see his family. She'd never been out of Nova Scotia, never been on a plane. She didn't have a passport and was intimidated by the prospect of navigating a strange city or foreign country.

Frustrated, Annie turned on her heel and walked out of the cottage. How could she explain her feelings to Rourke when she really didn't understand them at all? She trusted him completely and yet she couldn't trust herself. She was twenty-five years old and it was time to see a little more of the world.

Annie had managed to convince herself that a trip to New York City was exactly what she and Kit needed.

Rourke walked outside and found Annie sitting on the porch steps. "I'm sorry," she said. "As you can probably tell, I don't deal with change very well."

He sat down beside her, then grabbed her hand and pulled it to his lips. "I'm coming back. It's not like I'm leaving forever."

"I know," she said. "But it doesn't make things easier."

"Annie, I thought we were just in this for sex. That's what you said. That's what you continue to say. Has something changed?"

Annie felt a sliver of regret. She didn't want Rourke leaving without knowing how she really felt about him. But she'd never loved a man before, so she had no way of knowing whether these feelings were real or not.

She took a long, deep breath. "We're not just friends," Annie said.

"We aren't?"

"You mean everything to me," Annie said. "I

didn't want to need you, but I do. You've made my life so much better and I haven't thanked you."

Rourke slipped his arm around her shoulders and pulled her close, pressing a kiss to the top of her head. "I wouldn't leave if it wasn't really important."

"I understand," Annie said. "When do you have to go?"

"I thought I'd head out early tomorrow morning. It's a fifteen-hour drive and I can do it in a day if I leave early enough."

"I suppose you're going to want to get to bed early then," Annie suggested

Rourke grinned. "Are you trying to seduce me, Annie?"

"You don't take much convincing," she replied. "I can just smile at you and you seem ready to tear my clothes off."

"Then let's do it. I'll race you to the bed."

At first, she thought he was just teasing. But then she saw the desire in his eyes. Annie couldn't think of anything she'd rather do. With a soft sigh, she crawled onto his lap and wrapped her arms around his neck. "Promise me you'll come back."

"I promise," Rourke said.

"And promise, if there's another storm along the way, you won't stop and help another damsel in distress."

Rourke chuckled. "I'm beginning to think that was the smartest decision I've ever made."

Annie remembered that first night with him. From the moment she'd seen him, she knew she wanted him. He'd been so undeniably sexy and just his smile was enough to send shivers coursing through her body. That storm had changed her entire life. She was a different woman now, someone with the confidence to face the world on her own.

But now that she was ready, she didn't want to be alone. Annie liked having Rourke with her, close at hand. He seemed to belong in her house, as if he'd been with her all along. She'd never been one to dream about marriage and a family, but with Rourke, it seemed like a possibility.

"I'll race you to the bed," she said.

"I don't think so," Rourke said. He slipped his arm beneath her knees and around her back, then stood, picking her up as if she were as light as a sack of feathers. "Tonight, we're going to do everything very, very slowly."

Annie leaned close, brushing a kiss across his lips. Then she traced the same path with her tongue. Rourke groaned softly as he pulled the screen door open. A cool breeze blew through the cottage and streams of midday sunlight washed across the floor. With other men, Annie's desire had always cooled over time. But with Rourke, it only got more intense, threatening to consume them both.

He set her back on her feet next to the bed and then sat on the edge of the mattress, his hands removing her clothes, piece by piece. He lingered over each inch of flesh that he revealed, pulling her forward so that he could kiss her or caress her with his fingertips.

When she was finally naked, Rourke laid her back onto the bed, then slowly seduced her with his tongue. He found spots, both familiar and new, that sent wild sensations coursing through her body. Annie moaned softly when he found the place between her legs. Closing her eyes and tipping her head back, she lost herself in wave after wave of delicious pleasure.

He brought her to her release not once, but twice, and by the time she drew him up and guided him inside her, Annie was desperate to feel his body close to hers, to feel him drive into her with both gentleness and determination.

Though she hadn't said the words in his presence, there was no doubt in her mind that she was falling in love with Rourke Quinn. But at the same time, Annie knew she was risking her heart. Love didn't always last. And sometimes it wasn't a force for good, but a force for self-destruction. Would she be like her mother? Would love drive her to madness? Annie wanted to believe she was strong enough to weather the worst of any relationship, but how could she be sure?

"Tell me you love me," she whispered, her voice breathless, his fingertips skimming across her lips. She didn't care whether he meant it or not. She just needed to hear the words, to gauge her own reaction to them

"I do," Rourke murmured, his breath warm on her throat. "I love you, Annie."

She expected that familiar feeling, exhilaration mixed with dread, excitement mixed with terror. But to Annie's surprise, there was none of that. Instead, she felt a sweet sense of security, a quiet satisfaction, and more than anything else, a deep optimism that maybe this was meant to be.

ROURKE SAT IN the lawyer's office, staring down at his cell phone. He'd been in the city for three days and it looked as if it was going to take much longer than he'd originally anticipated to tie up the loose ends of his life and get back to Cape Breton.

He'd promised Annie that he'd call her and he made sure her cell phone was charged before he left. But he'd called her twice a day and hadn't gotten any response. No answer or callback, leaving him to wonder if she'd forgotten him already.

Though he thought he knew Annie well, it was still nearly impossible for Rourke to read her. She kept her emotions so carefully hidden and when she did display an extreme response, he was left to wonder what had caused it.

Women were complex creatures, that was true. But Annie gave new meaning to the word *complex.* Every day he'd managed to peel back another layer and Rourke thought he was getting closer to the real woman, the resilient woman at the core of her being, the woman with the barely healed scars.

He punched in her number again, then listened as it rang. She hadn't set up a voice-mail account, but she should be able to see that he'd called. Rourke cursed softly.

"Everything all right?"

He glanced up to see Maria sliding into her leather chair behind the desk. "Yeah. Fine."

"All right, I spoke yesterday to Ian Stephens, Aileen Quinn's representative in this estate matter. He explained to me that each heir will receive five hundred thousand dollars immediately and the other half of the inheritance after you've visited Miss Quinn in Ireland. She wants to meet her family members before she dies."

"Why is she giving away her money before she dies?" Rourke asked.

"From what I've read, Aileen Quinn has plenty of money."

Maria began to sort through the papers on her desk and Rourke watched her. At one time in his life, she was exactly his type—smart, confident, professional, with dark hair and a hot body. But as he looked at her now, he felt absolutely no attraction. God, was he really that hooked on Annie Macintosh?

Annie was odd, she was stubborn and there were times when she frustrated him to no end. And still, he couldn't stop thinking about her.

"All right. You just need to sign this, right by the tab."

Rourke did as he was told.

"And this at the bottom, with today's date."

When he'd finished signing all the documents, he pushed them across the desk to Maria. She handed him a letter. "This is from Mr. Stephens. You'll contact him and he'll make travel arrangements to Ireland for you. A visit is a requirement for the rest of the inheritance, so I suggest you make your plans soon. Miss Quinn is ninety-seven years old." Finally, she withdrew an envelope from a folder and held it out to him. "Congratulations," she said.

"Did you take your cut from this or will you bill me?" Rourke asked, opening the envelope to glance at the check.

"All the legal bills have been covered by Miss Quinn. I do have a gift for you," she said, reaching down to grab a small shopping bag. "These are a few of her bestselling books. I thought you might like to read them."

"Exactly how am I related to her?" he asked. "I don't recall my father or Buddy talking much about family."

"Through your grandfather Diarmuid Quinn. He was Aileen's older brother. He had three sons—your father, Paul, was the youngest. The eldest was Alistair. Both Buddy and Alistair fought in the Second World War. Buddy survived and Alistair died during the invasion of Normandy."

"My father never mentioned him. He barely mentioned his own father. Buddy never said anything about him either, except in passing. I got the impression that their childhood was not particularly happy."

"I only have the facts here," Maria said, "but I'm sure you could find out more with a little research."

Rourke stood and held out his hand. "Thank you. I don't think you know how much this means to me."

Maria smiled. "Are you free for lunch?" She paused as if unsure about what she was going to say next. "Now that you're no longer a client, I thought we could get to know each other better."

Rourke felt flattered, but he had absolutely no interest is this beautiful woman. "I can't," he said. "I'm actually involved with—I'm in love with someone else. And I need to get home because I've really been missing her."

"She's a lucky girl," Maria said, disappointment etched across her features.

"No," Rourke said with a chuckle. "I'm the lucky one."

He took her hand and shook it. "Goodbye. And thanks again."

"If you ever need any other legal help, please don't hesitate to call us."

Rourke strode out of the office. As soon as he got to the elevator, he pulled out his cell phone and dialed Annie once more. When she didn't answer, he decided to skip his next appointment and head back to the island.

The sooner he got to Cape Breton, the sooner he could get on with the rest of his life—a life that included Annie. He'd initially planned to stop by his father's old office to put Ed and his associates out of their misery. He had no intention of investing in a failing business, even if his father founded it and Rourke had given it eight years of his life. But he would agree to come on as a consultant, to try to help them turn things around. He owed that much to his father. He decided he could tell them that by phone.

He glanced at the time on his cell phone. It was nearly noon. Traffic was crazy in the city. If he drove straight through, he might be able to be back by dawn. He smiled to himself as he thought about slipping into the cottage and crawling into bed with Annie.

He hadn't slept well since he'd left her. Somehow, he needed her beside him or things didn't feel right. They were out of balance. His life was on the island right now and not anywhere else, not even in the city he'd called home for his entire life.

He found his SUV in a parking ramp two blocks from the lawyer's office. He was all packed up and ready to go. As he slipped into the truck, he loosened his tie then yanked it off. Closing the door behind him, Rourke sank back into the leather seat.

It hadn't really hit him until now, but this money had come at the perfect time. If he was careful with it, he'd never have to worry about a job again. It was enough for a lifetime with Annie.

Hell, he could have fallen in love with a girl who coveted eight-hundred-dollar designer shoes and dining in expensive Manhattan restaurants. Instead, he had Annie, who rarely wore shoes and preferred dried fruit and beans to fine cuisine.

As he was pulling out of the parking ramp, his phone rang. He glanced at the screen and recognized his mother's number. "Hi, Mom," he said.

"I just wanted to confirm our dinner plans," she said.

"Actually, I was about to call you. I'm going to head back to Cape Breton right now. I finished up with the lawyer and I'm just going to skip the meeting with Kopitski. There's nothing left to say. I'm not going back."

"You have so much money now. Why go back to Cape Breton at all?"

He didn't have the energy to explain it all to his mother. There would be hours of questions and a lot of answers he wasn't prepared to give. "There's a woman. And I'm pretty sure she's the one. And that's all I'm going to say for now, so don't ask for more, Mom. Listen, I'm trying to navigate traffic and I shouldn't be on the phone. I'll call you when I get back to Cape Breton. And don't obsess over this until I do. Her name is Annie."

"Annie," his mother said. "It's a nice name."

"It is. Bye, Mom." He shut off his phone and tossed it on the seat beside him. But almost immediately, it rang again. He picked it up and said, "Mom, I said no questions."

"Rourke?"

He didn't recognize the voice on the other end of the phone. "Yes?"

"Hi, it's Betty Gillies. I had a hard time tracking you down, but I found your number on one of our old orders. She doesn't know I'm calling but—"

"What's wrong?" he asked.

"I'm not sure what happened between you and Annie, but I thought you'd want to know."

"Nothing happened between us. I'm just in New

York for a few days. I'm headed back to the island right now."

"Well, for some reason, she refused to call you."

"What happened?"

"She was walking out on the rocks and slipped and broke her ankle. It was a terrible break. She splinted the break herself, made a crutch for herself and then dragged herself out to the road. Sam Decker found her and that dog of hers walking into town. She's in the regional hospital in Sydney now. They've done surgery on her ankle, but she's going to need some help when she gets home."

"I'm already on my way," Rourke said. "I should be there before dawn."

"Good. Maybe you can talk some sense into her. She doesn't seem to want to accept help—from anyone."

"Thanks for calling, Betty. I appreciate it."

He hung up the phone and swore to himself. This was exactly like the day he'd found her. And this was exactly why she should not be living all alone on Freer's Point. Like the day he found her lying in the rocks, her head bloody and her body cold, she'd managed to put herself in danger.

"That's never going to happen again," he muttered. "Not if I have anything to say about it."

9

ANNIE STARED AT the tray of food the aide had brought her for breakfast. Dinner last night had been some type of chicken with pasta salad and limp green beans. At least breakfast was food she could eat. Yogurt and granola and fresh fruit. She wondered if they'd let her order breakfast for every meal.

"How are we feeling this morning?" the nurse asked as she breezed into the room. "I thought I could help you to the bathroom if you're ready. You haven't gone since just after dinner last night."

"Actually, I have," Annie admitted. "I really don't need help. I was able to make it on my own."

"Miss Macintosh, the doctor does not want you moving around on your own. We've got a physical therapist coming in this morning to teach you how to get around on crutches. Once you've been cleared, then you can move around on your own. If this is a problem with you, we can always put you back into traction," she warned.

"I don't think that would help," Annie said.

"I see. And who are you going to have at home helping you."

"No one," Annie said.

"No one? I think you should call a family member or a friend. You need to rest. You've just had surgery."

"There's no one I can call," Annie said.

She'd been tempted to call Rourke all week, but after two days, she'd grown so frustrated with herself, she'd thrown her phone into the ocean. Annie had considered it a sign of weakness that she'd needed him so much. What had happened to her? Before he'd shown up, she'd been a strong, capable woman. Now, after a couple weeks together, she couldn't seem to survive without him.

"No one?" the nurse asked.

"No one," Annie said softly.

"Then I'll send in our home-care coordinator. She'll arrange for a visiting nurse to check in with you several times a day. And she'll help you find someone to work around the house, too."

"I don't—" Annie snapped her mouth shut. Maybe she ought to accept the help. Some of the folks in town had already offered to give her a hand when she got home. It seemed Sam Decker had spread the word about her injury. Having a stranger around was much easier than asking people she knew for help.

If Rourke were here, she could— Annie fought a surge of emotion. Ever since the surgery she'd been so weepy and all of the tears had been for Rourke. The doctor had said that was normal and that some patients experienced depression after hospitalization. But any hint of emotional weakness was enough to frighten Annie.

She had to be strong, she had to fight off the impulse to fall into self-pity. Though she wanted to believe that Rourke would come back, she knew that the pull of the city and his former life would be strong. Yes, he'd told her that he loved her, but it hadn't come naturally. She'd asked him for the sentiment.

Reaching for the carton of yogurt, Annie tried to ignore the empty spot deep inside her. She didn't feel complete anymore and she wondered when that void would disappear. Unlike food and water, sex—and Rourke—were not necessary to sustain life. It was possible to get along without him.

A knock sounded on the door and she sat up and caught sight of Sam Decker waiting outside. "If you want to get out of bed, ring the call bell," the nurse said.

As she left, Sam took a few steps inside. She hadn't seen him since he'd brought her—and Kit—

to the hospital. A wary smile curved his lips and Annie returned the smile "Hi," she said.

"How are you doing?"

"Good," Annie said. "How's Kit?"

"He's doing fine. He's staying over at the station and riding around with me on patrol. He likes sitting in the front seat and sticking his nose out the window."

"Thank you so much for taking care of him. I don't know what I would have done without your help."

Sam chuckled softly. "I never thought I'd hear you say something like that. You've never needed anyone's help, Annie."

She felt her cheeks warm with embarrassment. "I'm sorry, Sam. I'm sorry that I wasn't the kind of girl you needed. And I'm sorry if I took advantage of your feelings for me. That was wrong."

"You didn't take advantage," he said. "It's all my fault. I should have understood. The things that happened in the past didn't stay in the past."

"But they should have. You're a good man and I know that. I shouldn't have continued to judge you by things you'd done as a kid."

"I hope you always judge me, Annie. I hope you hold me to a higher standard than anyone else I know. And I want to live up to your expectations. That's what a good friend does."

"I hope we can be friends," she said.

"I'd like that." He paused. "I heard that Quinn is gone."

Annie nodded. "Yeah."

"Is he coming back?"

She shrugged, her gaze dropping back to her breakfast tray. "I don't know."

"I could always call him for you," Sam said. "If he loves you, Annie, he should be here with you."

"I know. I'll think about it. I really will." She drew a deep breath. "The doctor says I can go home later today, once they teach me how to walk on crutches."

"I'll come and take you home," Sam said. "Just ring the station and they'll get a message to me."

"All right."

"Hey, I better get going. Kit is down in the cruiser. He's already figured out how to turn on the siren. That dog is smart."

"Are you parked out front?" Annie asked. "Will you drive past so I can see him?"

"Sure. I'll see you later, Annie. I'm glad you're feeling better."

After he left the room, Annie threw back the covers of the bed and slid her feet to the floor. She wore a heavy plaster cast on her right ankle, making it hard to balance when she was standing. Searching for handholds, she hopped across the room to the window, then waited, staring out into the early-morning light.

A few minutes later, she saw Sam exit the hospital and waved at him. He caught sight of her and then jogged out to his cruiser, parked in a nearby emergency lane. When he opened the passenger-side door, Kit jumped out and circled excitedly around Sam's feet.

Annie laughed as Sam tried to get him to do a few tricks. Then he waved and they both got into the cruiser and drove off. Though he wasn't the man for her, she hoped that Sam would find a nice girl who'd appreciate him.

As she stared out the window, another figure caught her attention. She recognized the long, easy gait and the dark windblown hair. Her breath caught in her throat. "Rourke," she murmured.

She turned quickly and took a step toward the bed. But she lost her balance and pitched forward. The tray table was the only thing within reach and she grabbed for it. But she pulled it down on top of her, her breakfast dishes crashing to the floor with a loud clatter.

"Ow," she said, brushing a splatter of yogurt off her cheek.

A pair of nurses appeared at the door and she recognized the one who'd stopped by earlier. "What are you doing?" the nurse said, hurrying across the room to help her.

Annie forced a smile. "I really need you to help

me to the bathroom. I have to get this yogurt out of my hair."

"We'll get you a shower," the nurse said.

"No! There's not time for that. I have to get back into bed. Can you grab me a towel?"

ROURKE STOPPED AT the nurses' station and asked for Annie's room. The nurse pointed to his left and gave him the number, and he hurried down the hallway. He was anxious to make sure she was all right.

When he found the room, he knocked on the door, then slowly pushed it open. She was lying on the bed, her hair falling around her face, her leg encased in plaster.

A riot of emotions whirled in his head—frustration, relief, anger, elation. Anger came out first. "Why the hell didn't you call me? I find out you're in the hospital from someone else? Jaysus, Annie, I thought we were in this together. I thought we had something."

"I—"

He held up his hand. "I know you have a hard time trusting people, but it's me we're talking about here. The guy who loves you. The guy who wants to spend the rest of his life loving you. I think you could at least make an attempt to trust me."

"I—"

"I don't want to hear any silly excuses. If we're going to love each other, then this kind of behavior has got to stop."

"I—I do," Annie said.

"What?"

"I do trust you," she said. "And—and I do love you. And I'm sorry. You're right. I should have called you. As soon as this happened."

For a long moment, they stared at each other. Then, suddenly, emotion overwhelmed her. Maybe it was a reaction to the last of her walls tumbling down. Or maybe his anger had taken her by surprise. But she burst into tears, covering her face with her hands. Rourke hurried to the bed and gathered her in his arms.

"Hey, what's wrong? I'm here now. Everything is all right."

"I—I didn't think you were going to come back," she said.

"I called. Every day. Twice a day. Didn't you see my number on your display?"

She looked up at him through runny eyes. "I threw my phone in the ocean," she said.

"Why would you do that?"

"I was angry. Frustrated that I missed you so much. I didn't like how that felt."

He cupped her face in his hands and kissed her, his lips lingering over hers, his fingers brushing the tears from her cheeks. "I told you I'd be back."

"I—I know."

"Annie, if I say I'm going to do something, I'll do it." He pulled her into a fierce hug, pressing another kiss to the top of her head. "Are you all right?"

"Aside from being chronically weepy, yes, I'm fine. I broke my ankle." She paused, then frowned. "How did you know I was here?"

"Betty Gillies called me. She heard from Sam Decker. Let me tell you, I'm not so happy that he was the one who rescued you this time."

"You don't have to worry about Sam," she said. "We've come to an understanding. We're friends, nothing more."

"And he agreed to that?"

Annie nodded. "He did. And I think he finally accepts it."

"I'm not sure I do," Rourke said. "Maybe you can explain it to me."

"It was something that Sam said to me. He said if he could change, then why couldn't I? I think I have changed—inside. But I just haven't allowed myself to believe in those changes. I haven't allowed myself to be honest with you. I've been keeping something from you."

His expression turned cloudy and she reached out for his hand, weaving her fingers through his when she captured it. "I've always been afraid," she began. "Afraid that someday I'd turn out like my mother. And it's stopped me from living my life."

"Annie, just because—"

"Let me just say this," she interrupted. "I need to get it all out."

Rourke nodded, bringing her hand to his lips and kissing her wrist. "All right."

"If we spend our lives together, you have to understand that it might happen. My mother was bipolar. Manic-depressive. I may have inherited my mother's illness."

"And I may have inherited my father's heart disease," Rourke said. "I hope that doesn't change the way you feel about me."

"Of course not," Annie said.

"For better or worse. In sickness and in health," Rourke said. "Isn't that the way it goes?"

Annie drew a ragged breath, her tears threatening again. "Are you sure?"

Rourke slipped his hand around her nape and drew her into a long, lingering kiss. "Absolutely," he said.

"What does that mean?"

"That means I'm staying on the island. That means I intend to spend the rest of my life taking care of you—if you'll let me."

A smile broke through the tears and Annie laughed while another flood began. She waved her hand in front of her face. "Sorry, sorry."

"Don't be sorry, Annie. I'm here for the good times and the bad." He looked down into her eyes. "I love you. This time I'm saying it without prompting. I love you. And I'm ready to start a life with you here on Cape Breton."

She flung her arms around his neck. "I love you. I do. I know it. I feel it in my heart."

"When are you getting out of here?"

"This afternoon."

"Good. I'm taking you home to my place. If I have to play nursemaid, I'm going to do it with electricity and running water. And…" Rourke paused, frowning. "Where is Kit?"

"Sam has him. We can call him and he'll bring him over."

"Good. I'm not going to be happy until we're all together again." Rourke smiled down at her. "You are so beautiful. And I promise, even if I have to go away again, I'll always come back. And if you don't believe that, then I'm thinking we might want to get married."

Annie gasped. "Married?" She contemplated his offer for a long moment. "We're going to have to talk about that. I just want to spend the next few months in bed with you. We can leave those big decisions until later."

"Actually, I have to go to Ireland and meet my great-aunt. She just gave me a half-million dollars. And if I go visit her, she'll give me another half million."

Annie looked at him in disbelief. "Ireland? When?"

Rourke nodded. "Soon. But I promise to make it quick."

"No," Annie said, shaking her head.

"No?"

"No, don't make it quick. I—I want to go with you. I think I need to see a little more of the world. And I really don't want to let you out of my sight for now. So I guess we're going to Ireland?"

"We are," Rourke said.

"Could we wait until I have this cast off my leg? They're going to put a lighter one on in a few weeks."

"I think that could be arranged," Rourke said.

She smoothed her hand across his cheek. "You look tired."

"I drove straight through. Sixteen hours. I'm beat."

"Why don't you close that door and we'll have a nap," Annie suggested.

"A nap? You know what happens when we take a nap."

"Of course I do. That's why I suggested it."

Rourke did as he was asked, then kicked off his boots and crawled into the narrow bed with her. This was all he really needed out of life. This sweet, intoxicating woman in his arms, their life together just waiting for them. And all of this because of some quirk of nature that put a storm in his path.

Maybe it had been his destiny all along, to come back to Cape Breton and find her again. Fate was a strange thing, but he wasn't going to question his good fortune. He was simply going to give Annie the happiest future she could possibly have. That was his life and he was ready to live it.

Epilogue

"It's a beautiful tree," Ian Stephens said.

Aileen stood in front of the towering pine, sparkling with lights and ornaments. "It is, isn't it? I haven't had a tree in such a long time. As I got older, I preferred to avoid thinking about the holidays. But now that I have family coming to visit, we're decorating the entire house."

"I hope you're not exhausting yourself getting ready for this reunion you have planned," Ian said.

She slipped her arm through his. "Sally has hired some ladies from the village to come in and do all the decorating," Aileen said. "I just sit in a comfortable chair and tell them what to do." She chuckled to herself. Over the past year, Ian had come to know her quite well and she him. He'd brought her together with the descendants of two of her lost brothers and now he'd found Diarmuid's grandson, a young man living on Cape Breton Island in Nova Scotia.

But she would have to wait until Christmas to meet Rourke and his girlfriend, Annie. She'd talked to Rourke on the phone and he'd promised that they'd arrive a few days early for the reunion Aileen had planned and spend some time together before the rest of the family arrived.

"Come, Sally has set out our tea and she laid a fire in the library to take the chill out of the air. Let's settle in and you can tell me all about your search for Lochlan."

When they were both settled in front of the fire, Aileen poured the young man a cup of tea, then offered him a plate of ginger scones. "You've spent so much time working on this for me," she said. "What are you going to do if and when we're finally finished?"

"I don't know," Ian said. "I've finished up my doctorate in history. We're nearly done with your autobiography. And we have the documentary coming up. I have a few other research projects that I've put off, but after those, I don't have any plans."

"Perhaps you should take some time to relax," Aileen suggested. "You never speak about going out and having a bit of fun. When was the last time you had a date?"

A tiny smile curled the corners of Ian's mouth.

"It's been…a while. I suppose I've used work to avoid having any kind of social life."

"And why is that?" Aileen asked.

"There was a woman and we planned to get married, but then she met someone more exciting and ran off with him."

She took a sip of tea and studied the young man's face. "And so you just gave up?"

"I suppose you could say that," Ian murmured. "I just thought if I was patient, someone else would turn up. But I've been waiting three years."

"Hmm. Well, perhaps it's time to leap back on the horse and see where it takes you." She paused and winked at him over the rim of her teacup. "Of course, you'll do that after you find Lochlan."

"And what if I can't find Lochlan?" Ian asked.

"I have the utmost trust in you and your detective skills."

"Some people don't want to be found."

"Tell me," Aileen said, sensing that he'd discovered something.

"Unlike his brothers, Lochlan didn't leave Ireland. He lived in Dublin for a long time and ran afoul of the law several times. He married and shortly after, deserted his wife, taking all of her money with him. After that, he just disappears."

"There were no children?" Aileen asked.

Ian shook his head. "No. Not from that marriage. I'm afraid that your brother may have assumed another identity to avoid the authorities. If that's the case, then we might never find him."

"I suppose it is asking too much that we solve every mystery about my past," Aileen said. "Perhaps it's time to just let it go."

"No, I'm going to continue to look, at least until Christmas. It might take a touch of luck, but then we've been lucky all along. I know he's out there."

"He is," she said. "I can feel him. We could always hire a psychic. Hold a séance. Communicate with the dearly departed."

"We may need to resort to that," he said. "I have found a daughter of Lochlan's first wife. I'm going to meet with her in London and see if her mother passed along any information about her first husband. We can hope."

Aileen leaned forward and took his hand, pressing it between her palms. "I want to thank you," she said. "No matter what happens, you've changed my life and made an old lady very, very happy."

"I've enjoyed it," Ian said. "It got me out of the dusty old archives in the library. I'm going to be sad when it's finished."

"I think you need to write a book about Irish orphanages after the turn of the century. It's time to tell that story, now that it's become such a hot topic in the news."

"After listening to your stories, I know there

is a book there. But I'm not certain it would be a scholarly work."

"How do you mean?"

"I've always had the idea that I might like to write a novel."

"Oh, now, that would be a wonderful thing. I'm sure I could give you some advice. And when the manuscript is ready, I could pass it along to my agent. She certainly owes me a few favors. So does my editor, for that matter."

"I would be so honored," Ian said.

"Oh, it would be my pleasure, Mr. Stephens."

They chatted for most of the afternoon about Ian's future. And when she walked him to the door, Aileen knew that this handsome young man with dreams of becoming a novelist was as dear to her as any of her newly discovered relatives. It was time to call her solicitor and make arrangements for one more person to receive a portion of her estate.

Aileen waved to him as he drove away from the stone manor house. She hadn't written the last words of her own story. She would wait until they found Lochlan. And then she'd rest much easier. A chilly wind buffeted her body, cutting through the wool dress she wore.

"Another winter," she murmured. There was a time when winter frightened her, leaving her to wonder if she'd ever see the spring, ever watch the jonquils come up in her garden. But she wasn't afraid anymore. She had more than just her books to leave this world. She had a family. And they would remember her for many years to come.

* * * * *

Available October 22, 2013

#771 BACK IN SERVICE

Uniformly Hot!

by Isabel Sharpe

The girl whom injured airman Jameson Cartwright teased mercilessly in grade school has grown into a sexy, fun, vibrant woman. Kendra Lonergan wants to help him recover; he just wants her...in his bed!

#772 NO DESIRE DENIED

Forbidden Fantasies

by Cara Summers

Children's author Nell MacPherson has always had an active imagination. And with a stalker on her tail and sexy Secret Service agent Reid Sutherland in her bed, she's finding a whole new world of inspiration–the X-rated kind!

#773 DRIVING HER WILD

by Meg Maguire

When she retires from the ring, MMA fighter Steph Healy thinks she's left her toughest opponents behind her. Little does she know, a hapless, hot-blooded contractor will bring her to her knees....

#774 HER LAST BEST FLING

by Candace Havens

Macy Reynolds is looking for her big break, and she's hoping a scoop featuring Blake Michaels, the town's returning hero, will give it to her. Unfortunately, the hot marine has no intention of telling the sexy little newspaper publisher anything. But he'll *show* her....

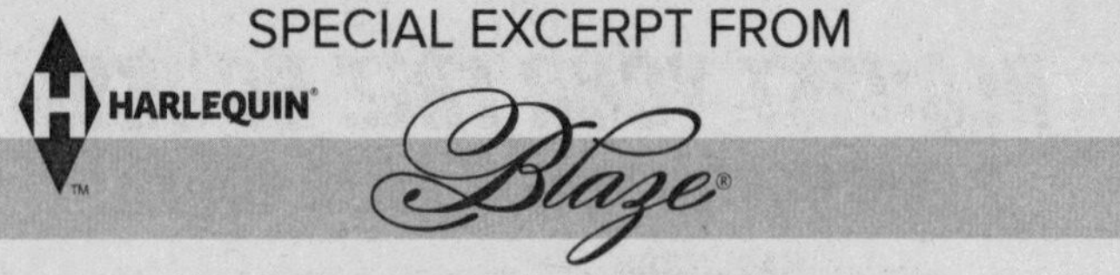

Cara Summers has a sizzling new FORBIDDEN FANTASIES story!
Here's a sneak peek at

No Desire Denied

"In one of my books, this would be a plot point. The characters would have to make a decision. Either they find out and deal with the consequences or they keep thinking about it. I would assume that in your job, it pays to know exactly what you're up against. Right?"

"Close enough."

But *he* wasn't nearly close enough. The heat of his breath burned her lips, but she had to have more. And talking wasn't going to get it for her. If she wanted to seduce Reid, *she* had to make the move.

Finally her arms were around him, her mouth parted beneath his. And she had her answers.

His mouth wasn't soft at all, but open and urgent. His taste was as dark and dangerous as the man. That much she'd guessed. But there was none of the control that he always seemed to coat himself with. None of the reserve. There was only heat and luxurious demand. She was sinking fast to a place where there was nothing but Reid and the glorious sensations only he could give her. She wanted to lose herself in them. Her heart had never raced this fast. Her body had never pulsed so desperately. Even in her wildest fantasies, she'd never

HBEXP79776

conceived of feeling this way. And it still wasn't enough. She needed more. Everything. Him. Digging her fingers into his shoulders, she pulled him closer.

Big mistake.

In some far corner of Reid's mind, the words blinked like a huge neon sign. They'd started sending their message the instant he'd told her they would settle what was happening between them now. He'd gotten out of the car to gain some distance, some perspective. Some resolve. But the brief respite had only seemed to increase the seductive pull Nell had on him.

He'd been a goner the moment he'd stuffed himself back into the front seat.

Long before that.

Oh, her argument had been flawless. Knowing exactly what you were up against was key in his job. Reid heartily wished it was her logic that had made his hands streak into her hair and not the feelings that she'd been arousing in him all day.

For seven years.

The hunger she'd triggered while she'd been talking so logically felt as if it had been buried inside him forever. Then once her lips pressed against his, he forgot everything except that he was finally kissing her. Finally touching her hair. He hadn't imagined how silky the texture would be. One hand remained there, trapped, while the other roamed freely, moving down and over her, memorizing the curves and angles in one possessive stroke.

HBEXP79776